DARKEST DAYS

BOYD CRAVEN III

To be notified of new releases, please sign up for my mailing list at:
http://eepurl.com/bghQb1

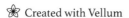

PROLOGUE

There comes a time in every man's life when he makes a mistake, he's not sure he can live with. I've reached that point in my life, and I know every decision that got me to this moment. If I could have done everything over, I didn't think I would have, or could have, changed what had ended up happening. Something dark, like fate, or Murphy, had a heavy hand controlling events. I had ended up going back to the farm where the little kids were... I'd had to do it. I had killed or been the reason for their father's deaths as much as the fathers themselves. I couldn't stand by and know in my heart that they would be taken and used by men of evil intent, or worse—starve, alone, not knowing.

So, I'd gone back, I'd done what I could. It hadn't been enough. Not even close to being anywhere near close enough. Emily and Mary had been kidnapped by Lance's crew, despite everything. I'd done my damnedest to break them out, catching a bullet and getting my skull cracked in the process. Jessica had been burned trying to save the prisoners that the Hill-billy Mafia was starting to stockpile, and I'd managed to piss off almost all of her entire group.

To make matters much, much worse, I found out her family was in a precarious position with Henry, the real leader behind the MAG group they were part of. They were worried about losing their place in an area that Henry had leased—on paper at least. I didn't think it mattered now that TSHTF, but they did. I was effectively a prisoner until I'd made the choice to do something about it. Henry had lied and was going to hold me, Raider, Emily and Mary until I had been indentured to them long enough. He'd lied about the reasons, and he'd lied about having my grandparents protected; he'd lied about everything.

I'd sicced my dog on him instead of catching a bullet. In the interim, several people had been shot, two of them by me and one by Jessica's father, Dave. In my bid to protect myself and my freedom, I made a horrible mistake, one I don't know if I can live with. Losing her, it guts me, and I'm not sure if I'll survive this mistake.

I'd pulled the trigger once, in the same heartbeat David had fired. Almost simultaneously I'd felt something hit me, whether it was physical or mental. Did I pass out? I couldn't have passed out, I was dreaming. But the dreams didn't stop the memory. My shot had gone through, just as Jessica jumped in front of her father, screaming. Her head had snapped backward, and both of them fell spinning, as if in slow motion. Dave's gun went off again as he fell, and in my peripheral vision, I saw Mary fall, scarlet exploding from her throat. Blood everywhere, the smell of iron, cordite, and evacuated bowels.

Dead.

I wanted to be dead. Maybe I was dead. Maybe I was dreaming, maybe this didn't happen. I prayed this hadn't happened. This was hell. I was in hell.

"HE'S COMING TO," I heard a voice say as something acrid assaulted my nose.

"It's about time. Get him tied up," Henry's voice snarled.

I opened my eyes as two sets of hands were roughly picking me up by my shoulders. Jimmy's hands were strong, and I felt my shoulder sockets ready to crumble, my injured shoulder screaming in pain.

"Don't make it worse," Carter yelled, bumping his massive chest into Jimmy's side.

"I ought to drop him down the hill," Jimmy said, his voice full of emotion.

"Jimmy, we don't have time for this. I need to get to work on the ladies with Duke."

"I said lock him up," Henry yelled, his voice shrill, "and somebody shoot this damned dog."

My eyes opened, and I focused them. Jimmy and

Carter had gotten me to my feet. Henry's arm was crimson where Raider's teeth had sunk in deep, his entire arm hanging loose at his side. Raider was sitting between me and the leader of the local militia, at attention.

"Nobody is shooting the dog," Carter said, drawing a handgun and holding it at his side. "And if anybody is going to get locked up here, it's both you *and* Wes until we get things sorted out."

Henry was flabbergasted. I noted his gun was laying between Raider's paws. The two men saw me looking, and I felt Jimmy's hold on me loosen.

"Henry, you're coming with me," Carter said, walking over and roughly jerking Henry, almost off his feet.

He pushed the older man face first against the wall and did a quick frisking, throwing things behind him. A spare pistol at the small of his back and several knives, including a small folder that he had in one of the cargo pouches of his pants. If I wasn't so horrified by what had happened, I might've enjoyed the show. He'd lied, he lied, and he was responsible as much as me for the injuries here today. What had happened to me? After I'd fired my gun, I'd fallen. Passed out, hit my head?

"Wes, you better come with me. Don't give me any problems. There's a way too much tension going on right now," Jimmy said, holding onto one shoulder as if to steady me.

2

"Raider," I said harshly as if to call him to my side. "What have I done?"

The last was directed toward Jimmy as much as it was for me. Raider stood, looked at the gun and then looked back at us before running to my side. He pushed his big head under my hand and then licked my wrist. Carter was pulling on my shoulder, but I looked at the area where the shooting had taken place. There was a form crumpled on the floor, and it wasn't Henry who was going into fits as Carter used his strength to hold him still. It looked like Jess' father, Linda's husband, was on the floor. A large hole had been opened just above the jawline behind his eye.

It was gruesome, and I didn't linger long, looking at the body. There was more blood on the ground in a different area, it'd been obvious that it'd been stepped through and someone with bloodied hands had been crawling around. The bloody handprints were the first evidence I saw, but to my left was what really had me scared. It looked as if someone turned on a hose, but instead of water the contents were red droplets, sprayed all over the polished concrete floor. They were now starting to dry, turning a brownish color.

"Where's Jessica?" I asked as Jimmy tugged at me again, leading me toward the stairs.

"Duke's performing surgery, and if Carter can handle Henry there..."

"Henry, dammit," Carter said, squeezing the man then using his bulk to push Henry against the block wall. "If you don't knock it off—" He holstered his pistol to use both hands to hold the struggling man.

"You're out of here, you're all out of here," Henry said, his words a snarl.

"You can't throw anyone out," Carter told him, "and we're all going to have a town hall meeting over what happened here today. I wouldn't be surprised if *you're* the one thrown out of here, so if you don't stop fighting me, I'm gonna bash your brains in."

Henry went silent for a moment and then tried once more to break out of Carter's grip. Carter squeezed harder and pushed Henry into the wall with a sudden burst of speed. There was a sickening thud as his head hit first, and Henry dropped bonelessly to the ground. Carter knelt over him, feeling for a pulse and then pulled out zip ties from a pouch in his belt. Once he was secure, he picked him up over one shoulder and motioned for Jimmy to start moving.

Jess was in surgery, but she was alive. I'd seen her take the bullet. I'd seen her head snap back. What about Mary, what about the little girl? And Emily, where had she gone? There had been a lot of people in the room when I'd fired that bullet, but where did everyone go? Why had I lost so much time again?

I WAS PLACED INTO ONE OF THE BEDROOMS ON THE FIRST floor that Jessica had pointed out to me before. It actually was just an empty 10 x 10 room with a secure door that was locked behind me. I heard the door next to mine open and shut and someone work the lock as well. At least I had Raider, at least I had my buddy. Everything was going dark and fuzzy around the edges again. Was this anxiety, panic, had I hit my head again? I didn't know; I had lots of questions but no answers. My face felt chapped, and I reached a hand up feeling the wetness on my cheek. I looked at it, seeing that my hand was damp, and realized that I had been crying for some time now.

Somewhere I heard a radio go off, and I could hear a woman screaming. Was it Jessica, Linda, Emily, Mary? I sat in a corner and put my back against the wall. Raider came over and pushed his head under my left arm. I heard voices talking, men's voices. And then I realized I'd heard something I hadn't been expecting: a vent fan had come on, and warm air was blowing into my face. I looked up at the drop ceiling that had been installed here and saw that there was a four-inch plastic vent that had been put in place.

The sounds became more muted with the fan blowing, but I strained to listen anyway. Raider pushed himself further until I finally let my legs go down flat on the concrete floor, and he crawled into my lap, the way he used to when he was a lot smaller.

"She's alive, buddy," I told my dog. "Thank you for what you did. I might've screwed everything up here. She has to be okay. She has to be okay."

Raider made a chuffing sound through his nose and then rubbed his big head against my chest. I worked my fingers through the fur on his neck, relaxing him as much as me, and listened. The screaming stopped, the voices were muted. For the first time in a while, I closed my eyes, let the tears come, and prayed to God.

2

I WOKE up to someone knocking on the door. Carter was there, and he had smears of dried blood on his temple and cheek. He had two metal folding chairs in one big hand, and he opened the door with the other. He came inside, let the door shut behind him, and it locked itself with a click. Raider stood and stretched, and at the same time he growled. His guard hairs started standing up along the ridge of his spine. Carter took a step back, so his back was to the door and put the chairs in front of him.

"Easy big guy, I'm in here to give news, I'm not here to hurt your buddy."

"What's the news?" I asked, my voice feeling raw and scratchy.

"How much do you remember?" Carter asked me.

"Too much," I said softly. "Tell me how everyone is doing. Are Mary and Jessica okay?"

Carter just looked at me for a moment and then

grunted, looking at his feet. "Aren't you even going to ask about Linda?"

"I don't know," I admitted. "I know Henry was blackmailing them, I know he lied to all of you to try to keep me here, but when he pulled... When Dave pulled a gun and was going to shoot my dog, I had no choice."

"You really think ... you really value your dog's life more than a human's?" His words were soft, almost thoughtful sounding.

"Raider, stand down," I commanded, and Raider sat next to me. I didn't answer his question, letting my silence be all the answer he needed.

I motioned for Carter to come closer, which he did. He watched my dog warily, and then undid one of the big folding chairs and sat. He opened another one and put it across from him. I was still sore all over, but I made it to my feet on my own and pulled the chair back against the wall then sat facing him. When we were both sitting and staring at each other, he bit the side of his cheek and then nodded.

"Dave's shot ricocheted. The piece that hit Mary had flattened out and acted almost like a knife. The cut in her jugular was bad, but if Duke hadn't been where he was, we would've lost her. He was able to get a finger on the bleed, and you know how we are here—we have just about everything we need in a pinch. Between Duke and I, we were able to get the cut sewn shut. She lost a lot of blood, Westley. I can't even tell you how much blood that little girl lost, but she's hanging on right now. I don't know if she'll make it, but without knowing her blood type and finding her some more blood, it's going to be touch and go. We're pumping her up full of fluids to bulk up the volume, but..."

"So little Mary's alive?" I asked rhetorically. "What about Jess? I heard you say she was in surgery."

"Wes, what you have to understand is you were already falling backward as you pulled the trigger. I don't know why you were collapsing or passing out, but your bullet traveled on an upward trajectory. It went in through one side of Jessica's cheek and out the other side, taking several teeth. Her father caught the rest of the lead in the face. Her entry wound was really easy to repair. Duke and I had to use some of the anesthetic you made for us to halfway knock her out. We were able to get the broken sections, the shattered remains of the tooth and some of the bone, out of the exit wound. We sewed her jaw the best we could, and we got the other cheek cleaned up as well."

"When can I see her?"

"Right now, your safest place to be is right here. I know you've been needling Linda Carpenter, and she might even deserve some of it from what I've been hearing about everything. But you just killed her husband and shot her baby girl in the face."

"That's the last thing I wanted to do, but I'm so glad she's okay," I said softly, feeling moisture running down my cheek again.

"Actually, though, I'm not here to give you news, more like ask a question. What's your blood type?"

"Why? I thought you didn't know her blood type?" I said, thinking of Mary.

"I want to find out, but Emily won't talk to us. I want to bring her here, with you. I want to see if you can find out Mary's type. She's..."

His words trailed off, but his big hands were folded together, and he was staring at his shoes. She was probably in a rage, probably half mad from wondering whether her daughter was alive or dead. I was already nodding as he had been explaining it, but he looked up and then nodded back at me.

"I'll be back with her soon. I'm to leave the chairs in here. No matter what happens, stay away from Linda. Henry's not the only one who wants you dead right now."

I felt horrible, but I nodded in agreement. I'd never wanted to kill him, but I'd never wanted him to kill Raider either. The chair protested as he got up, and he headed to the door. Two quick steps and he was gone. The door clicked shut behind him, and I heard what sounded like a deadbolt being thrown from the other side. I hoped Linda didn't have a key, almost as much as I hoped Jessica could forgive me. I was tired—Lord, I was tired—and nauseated. Raider was sitting by my side, and I heard his stomach grumble. Mine grumbled back, almost as a response. How could I be hungry at a time like this?

I WAS ZONING OUT, ALONE IN THAT ROOM, AND I HAD NO idea how long I waited, but I could hear Emily screaming and cursing long before I saw her. There was a sharp knock at the door, and then I heard the locks being thrown before it opened, and Emily was pushed through. She was cursing and screaming, almost spitting with rage, clawing at the closing door. I heard the locks once again, and she turned around and saw me. Her eyes went wide, and she took two quick steps, reaching for the folding chair. She'd quit cursing, and something calm seemed to have come over her. When she picked the chair up and raised it over her head, Raider let out a surprised bark, and I rolled out of the way as the chair came crashing down on the spot where I had been sitting just a moment before.

Raider let out a yelp and then a growl. He made half of a rush at Emily, growling, snarling, and barking. The echoing of the walls made him sound like he was demonically possessed.

"Emily, dammit."

I was already dodging to my right when the chair came crashing down again. I grabbed onto Raider's collar and pulled him back as well, until we were in the corner I'd fallen asleep in earlier.

"Emily wait, it's me Wes." I was almost begging.

I pulled Raider into my lap and leaned over, fighting to hold him down, covering him with my head and shoulders and my arms around him. He didn't like

11

that, and he wanted to protect me. I got a painful bite on my arm but held on. He didn't break the skin, but he was definitely letting me know he didn't appreciate what I was doing.

"I'm going to kill everyone here," Emily snarled, "if my little girl dies."

"Emily, don't."

"The only person who's not to blame here is me," she said, the chair raised over her head.

She was close enough that there was no more dodging. I'd seen people hit in the head with folding chairs on television. I was afraid of the small woman, I suddenly realized. Her arms tensed as she started to swing, and then she just dropped the chair behind her and melted to the floor sobbing.

I let Raider's collar go as he was already fighting to get away. Watching her fall apart broke something in me, and I started sobbing as well. What had I done? I didn't even begrudge my buddy for the bite; I deserved that and everything worse. I had shot Jessica in the face. I'd killed her father. My anger over her parents refusing to help the people at the crater... David's attempt to shoot my dog on top of everything else... I'd worn that anger and self-right-eousness like a cloak, and now it was all ashes. I'd crossed a line. A little girl was near death. That thought, more than anything else, got my sobs under control.

Raider was sitting between Emily and I, very alert. Now that Emily didn't have a chair over her head in a baseball swing, he merely looked at her, his hair no longer on end.

"...let me out of here!" I heard Henry's voice from close by.

Emily's head jerked to the side he came from, and she spat at the wall before scooting to me. She'd seen me at my lowest point—when I was weak, when I was vulnerable. She crawled into my lap and put her arms around me. I hesitated a second and put my arms around her as she fell apart again. Raider came over almost immediately and tried pushing between us. I loosened my grip and let him. Emily was trying to say something, but the words were lost to the sobs, the running nose, the mass of hair covering her face, her words on my shoulder.

Raider, being the diplomat he was, backed up in exasperation and barked, then started licking the side of her face.

"I'm going to boot all of you!" Henry screamed, then made a couple of urking sounds, like he was vomiting.

"Emily," I said, pushing her gently off my lap and getting some space as Raider tried pushing in the middle again, "what is Mary's blood type? They need to know that."

"They said there wasn't anyone here with her blood type," Emily said, the first thing I'd understood.

"What's her blood type?" I repeated.

"AB Negative."

I got up, careful not to knock her over. The room

looked like a tornado had gone through it. We had been in the corner, but the chair she'd used to try to bludgeon me was bent out of shape, flakes of paint from the chair marred the floor. Emily looked at me, wiping the tears and snot away with one arm as I banged on the door.

"Westley?" Carter asked.

"My blood type is B Negative, Emily is AB Negative," I called loudly.

"Dead, you're all dead," Henry hollered again, before falling silent.

"I'm unlocking the door," Carter yelled.

Emily had gotten to her feet at some point and was just behind me, still sniffling. It was Raider who made himself known, though, because as the deadbolts were undone, he pushed his head under my hand, so my hand ended up resting on his back. Every guard hair was standing on end, and a low growl was coming from deep within his chest. After a moment, the door swung open showing Carter and Jimmy standing there. Carter had his pistol by his side, drawn but pointing down.

"You're B Negative?" he asked again.

"Yes," I confirmed. "Emily—"

"Mary's AB Negative," she said, her voice small behind me.

"We're not going to have any problems with you, ma'am, are we?" Carter asked her, looking over my shoulder.

"Help my baby, please."

"Carter? Jimmy? Linda? Let me out of here!"

Henry's yell was punctuated by somebody kicking the door.

Carter handed Jimmy his pistol and nodded at the door that was being kicked. "If Henry kicks open that door, shoot him."

"I ... ok," he said, looking unsure.

"We don't have much time, Emily and Wes. You two behave, Mary's life depends on it."

I nodded and followed the big man.

THE ROOM I'd been mixing chemicals in had been quickly cleaned and turned into a surgical theater. I could smell the sharp bite of a bleach solution that they'd used to sanitize and wipe down things, and Duke was washing his hands in a sink spotted with red and brown. Blood, new and old. Two forms were laying on mats under green wool blankets. The larger one was moving, moaning, crying. The smaller one was still. Too still and too small. Emily started crying behind me, her head leaned against my right shoulder, and I paused in the doorway to take it all in.

Raider ran ahead of me, but stopped between the ladies, looking from one to the other.

"We can't afford an infection—"

"Raider, come," I said, patting my leg and walking in, followed by Emily and then Carter.

"Ma'am, it's good to see you calm. As you can see, we have your daughter stabilized right now; she's sleeping off the shock. I'm giving her saline to bulk out her blood, but unless—"

"They're a match," Carter interrupted, pushing me back gently, then pulling on my shirt sleeve. I started to help, but then pulled it off over my head.

My skin prickled as goose bumps covered my arms and chest. I held out both arms. Duke looked me over hard and then walked up. His big hand wrapped around my elbow as he was checking the veins.

"You pass out easily?" he asked me.

"Yes, he just had a TBI, a cracked skull, and we don't know why he passed out when the action happened."

"Right," Duke grunted, then looked at the office chair I'd rolled in here the last time I was mixing chemicals and pointed for me to sit.

The fake leather was freezing. It was probably the same temperature as the air, but it felt like ice against my back. The bag of solution going into Mary was hung on the wall by a nail, gravity doing the trick. Duke tied a rubber strap around my arm and made me make a fist. I heard what sounded like a clearing of a throat and looked over at Jess, who pulled the blanket back from her face a little bit.

"Are you?" the words came out funny, as if she was talking through a mouthful of cotton.

Her left cheek had a small puckered hole that had been sewn shut, but her right cheek looked like somebody had taken a knife to it in a star pattern and then sewed it shut.

"No," I said as I felt the needle pierce my arm.

I tried not to flinch, but Duke's big hand held me down. Carter was working quickly, hooking up lines and what looked like a small white box with blinking lights and numbers.

"Let go of your fist," Duke said, putting a piece of tape over the IV line and then untying the rubber strap.

I felt cold. I watched the blood fill the line for a moment, then looked over at Jess.

"I'm sorry." I felt stupid saying the words, but I was out of anything slick.

"My dad?" Her words were slow, thick, but getting stronger despite the tears.

I looked between Emily and the two men in the room. They all looked away. Emily put her hand on my bare shoulder. I shuddered as her warmth made my skin break out into goose bumps all over again. Jessica moved her eyes looking at the guys, at Mary's still form, then back at me. I looked down to meet her gaze and shook my head.

"He's dead?" she asked, her voice louder with a quiver I didn't like.

I nodded, my throat dry. Raider pushed between Emily and me, pushing his head under my right hand, petting himself. I worked my fingers through the thick coat.

"Why?" she asked me, her voice almost deathly silent.

"Because Henry was going to kill Wes, and your

dad was going to shoot Raider. Wes took a shot, but you jumped in the middle. Didn't stop your father from shooting my daughter in the throat!" Emily was coming unglued again, her fingernails biting into my shoulder.

I reached up and grabbed her wrist hard, hard enough I could feel the bones starting to grind, until she looked down at me. "Don't," I told her. "This isn't the time."

"When the hell is?" Emily shrieked.

"When your daughter is up and around," Duke said, his voice loud and filled with anger.

I listened as Carter started explaining to Emily how the transfusion was going to work, but my mind drifted. I wasn't ready to consider the actions I'd taken and the consequences of them. My grandparents had been left vulnerable, and I'd only wanted to get away. A booming bark made Raider twitch, and he let out a long vocalization that sounded like it had a lot of r's and wu wu wu, something I hadn't heard before. Another bark and scrabbling of claws could be heard over Henry, who'd started screaming to be let out again.

Then I heard a harsh command growled from outside the door. Linda stepped inside, flanked by Diesel & Yaeger.

"Linda, I can't have more dogs in here!"

Raider was making that sound again, and I realized that he was asking something. Of whom, I didn't know, but he pulled away from me and went to the others.

"I'll take them outside," Linda said softly, a different woman than the one who'd used Jess' command to stop the dogs from gang piling everybody.

"Don't," Carter said.

"Why?" she asked.

I looked at the red flow of blood. It was slow and progressing down toward the child. Did I have enough? Was it clean? All the moonshine, the previous infection... I realized my head was scrambled, and I wasn't thinking clearly.

"Your ... husband..." Carter said but couldn't finish the words.

"We can't have all three dogs in here," Duke repeated. "We need to keep this area as sanitary as we can. We just performed a meatball surgery. Take them somewhere else."

Emily was agitated. Her hands kept running up and down her arms, and she was shifting from foot to foot. I knew the madness that was driving her, but the small woman had shown me a savagery I'd never have guessed. She kind of scared me, and if I could fix this, fix her little girl, I would do whatever it took.

"I meant, I'll take them outside of this room." Linda was crying. "Jess..."

"I'm here, Mom," Jess said, pulling the blanket back and sitting up.

Linda flinched, but it was a small thing, barely noticeable. "I'm..." Then she was moving to her daughter, sitting next to her and wrapping her in her arms. Raider walked to the door, and the dogs started sniffing each other in greeting. Yaeger ignored the eager rambunctiousness of my pup, but Diesel looked like he was coiled, ready to spring, pounce...

"I'll take the three dogs," Carter said, moving past everyone. "I'm not really needed here at the moment, am I?"

"I've got things handled," Duke said, "but when you can, check on Jimmy and Henry. We need to have a town hall, and pretty damn quick, but..." His words trailed off as he saw something in the plastic tubing and started playing with things.

"I'm going to need you to move up onto the counter," Duke told me, putting a hand under my arms.

Raider growled, but I made a shushing noise and let the big man help me to my feet. Once again, he showed his immense strength as he simply hoisted me onto the counter like I was a toddler being picked up by his parent.

"Now lay down and hold still." His words were soft.

"Is she going to be ok?" I whispered to him, knowing half the room probably had heard my question.

"Who?" he asked.

"Mary," I said, my eyes heavy.

"She's lost a lot of blood. Her body's in shock. This helps, a lot, but I don't know if it's going to be enough." He whispered so quietly that I knew it was meant only for me.

"Take as much as you need," I told him, grabbing his arm tightly to make my point. "Save her."

Duke looked at me for a moment, and something softened in his expression as he nodded. I let go and got comfortable, my head turned to the side, watching the red make its way to the girl. Most of this was gravity, but they had this down pat. I tried to work out in my mind how it was working. I heard feminine sobs and turned to see three figures sitting on the floor under Jess' blanket, staring at Mary. Linda, Jess, and Emily. The women were holding each other, murmuring to each other. I had caused this. I was the source of the grief.

"You should sleep," Duke said after checking on Mary's vitals. "I won't let you roll off. I can see how you've been fighting exhaustion, and you've just recovered for the most part."

I nodded and let my mind wander. I fought off the depression as best as I could. I wanted Grandma's lemonade. I wanted...

4

I FELT somebody washing my face. I pushed gently so I could open my eyes and realized it wasn't somebody, but something. Or several somethings. Raider let out an excited bark, and I opened my eyes. I had been placed in the closet room I'd been in before. Raider was by my side, giving me his goofy doggy smile. I remembered waking at some point and Duke unhooking the IV, somebody helping me down the hallway, but my mouth was dry, and my head ached. I could see somebody standing in the doorway, the gloom blocking their features.

"Who let you in?" I asked him, sitting up.

"I did," Grandma said from the chair at the foot of the bed.

It startled me, but I sat up quickly. My head swam, but it wasn't as bad as it had been. Grandpa walked into the room, and I was crushed between both of them. Raider kept pushing his snout between us as I laughed, cried, hugged them and tried to form a coherent string of words. I couldn't. Joy. Bliss. My family was safe, they were right here!

"Not to be a spoil sport," Carter said from the hallway, "but you need your rest. We uh ... took what we needed," he said, not meeting my gaze when I turned to face him.

"Mary?" I asked.

A small smile touched his lips, and he gave me a nod. I sat back on the cot, only to be almost thrown off when first Grandpa then Raider landed on the other end. It was nearly a tangle, but my heart was leaping with Joy.

"Jessica and Emily?" I asked.

"Jessica's going to need a dentist someday I think, but she should recover fine. We'll have to watch for infection. Emily is with Linda, they're ... burying David."

I puzzled over that. I knew some of the madness that drove Emily, but I'd seen her come completely unhinged when her daughter was knocking on death's door. Somewhere in the room earlier, they had all made up? Had to have.

"Thank you for everything," I told Carter, who hesitated a moment more.

"It almost wasn't good for everyone. Duke had to remove Linda from the room near the end there. She tried to..." he stalled.

"What's the matter? Cat grabbed your johnson?" Grandma asked.

24

Grandpa and I let out a surprised bark of a laugh at the same time, but Carter was serious. "You told Duke to do whatever it took to save Mary. He did, but near the end, Linda and Jess thought it was too much."

"I told him—"

"I know, and he was going to do it that way, but Mary woke up first."

"Wait, she's awake?" I asked, standing again, feeling my head swim.

"If you promise to take it easy, the three of you can come with me."

"Best damned news I've heard all day!" Grandpa said, standing, smacking me in the chest with his free hand before rubbing them together.

"How did you two—"

"Let's go see the little girl," Grandma interrupted.

Avoiding the topic. I'd have to revisit it later.

Carter showed us to the living room area instead of where we'd been earlier. Diesel was laying at the head of the couch, a blanket draped over his side. Laying on him, as if he was a meat pillow, was little Mary. She had been changed and looked like she'd been scrubbed clean. At her feet was Yaeger. Kneeling in front of her, her hands together in prayer, was Jess. Both looked up as the four of us approached.

"They wouldn't let me help, so I decided to watch over her." Jess looked up, and her face was tear streaked.

Grandpa and Grandma settled into the couch on the other side, and I sat on the floor near Jess. She scooted some to give me room. I was expecting to see Mary's eyes closed in a restful, healing sleep. Instead, she was sitting there, her eyes open. She held out her hands to me. I gave her mine, and she held it in both of hers. Her hands were tiny, soft. She turned my hand over and used a fingernail to trace the lines on mine. Then she squeezed. I looked into her eyes.

"Thank you," she said, her voice harsh and raspy.

"Shhh, honey, Duke said you shouldn't talk."

There was bruising on her throat, as if a big hand had clamped down on the side of her neck, and I realized it had. Duke had used his size and strength to prevent as much bleeding as he could. In the process, he'd probably bruised up the insides of her throat too.

"I'm sorry," I said softly, putting my head down on the couch, uncomfortably close to Diesel's big feet and near eye level for the little girl. "I was just trying to get home, get you and your mom safe, get to my grandparents. I never meant for anybody to get hurt."

She gave my hand a squeeze and a slow exhausted smile. Then she let go with one hand and held it out to Jess. Jess did the same thing I did and gave Mary her hand. Mary held mine and Jess' at the same time for a moment, then put her hands together, putting Jess' and mine together. She moved her small hands to our fingers and gave us both a squeeze before letting go. Jess' fingers intertwined with mine, and we sat there. I looked into her eyes and saw anger, hurt, fear, and something more tender. I broke my gaze to look at Mary, to see if she'd meant to do that on purpose, but her eyes were closed. Her chest rose and fell as she breathed through her throat softly, making a purr as she fell asleep.

"I don't know about you, but I need a drink," Grandpa said, hoisting himself out of the couch, pulling a flask from the middle pocket of his bib.

"I do," I told him, reaching for the flask.

"You will not drink the potent stuff. Here..." Grandma was digging in her big carryall purse. She pulled out a well-worn and familiar thermos and took the cap off, handing it to me. I turned it over to use as a cup as she spun off the inner cap.

I held it out, and she poured. The special lemonade filled the small area with its sweet but tart aroma. I drank the cup greedily, feeling the alcohol hit my system in a slow burn. It had been a while, and when I held my cup out, Grandma was ready. When she was done pouring, she put the inner cap back on, knowing I would have held the cup out for thirds. Grandpa ignored both of us and was taking sips from his flask. Jess tried to grin, but her cheek pinched as the pain stopped her.

"I'm sorry," I told her after gulping down the second cup.

"Not now," she said softly, then turned back to Mary and started running her hands through her hair.

I wanted to do the same with both of them, but instead, walked over to the couch Grandpa had been sitting at a moment before. My grandparents joined me as we watched Jess and Mary.

"I was getting concerned when you hadn't come home. They said it could take a while, so I had Grandpa put your truck back together," Grandma said, putting the thermos into her purse.

She'd dressed for travel. When she was around the house, she dressed differently. Market days and shopping days, she'd put on a nicer dress, and pull her hair into a bun, and she had a set of glasses she never wore around the house unless she was reading.

"They just let you in?" I asked.

"A group like the first time found us on the trail. I think I found some sort of motion-activated alarm, but I'm not sure. They got to us so quickly—" Grandpa was saying when Grandma interrupted, "And I told them to bring me to my grandson, or there would be hell to pay. So they brought us here."

"I heard some of what happened," Grandpa said, looking to the stairwell that led up. "Jess, I'm sorry about your father."

"Not now, ok?" Jess said shortly, pulling her hand from mine. "Wes, you'll watch Mary for a bit?"

"I'll stay right here," I told her, watching as she got up and wiped her eyes.

Raider pushed his head against my leg, and I reached down to pet him. I wobbled, then decided to sit. The alcohol was hitting me already, but it gave me a warm feeling inside. I sat next to Mary, then turned and stretched my legs out facing my grandparents as Jess walked upstairs, probably to join her mother and Emily.

"What happened?" Grandma asked me softly.

"Henry ... I ... I don't even know where to start. Apparently, he's the guy who holds the lease for this tract of land. He was kind of blackmailing Jess' parents, and he was trying to do the same thing with me. I played along for a little while, but I was planning on getting out of here. They said I had to work off what they'd used to make me better—medicine, labor, and food. He decided he was gonna tack Emily and Mary to my bill. I'd had enough and tried to leave."

"How did you end up killing Jess' dad?" Grandma asked.

"When I went to leave, Henry pulled a gun on me. He would have shot me if I'd tried to get away from the group. I timed the moment right and sicced Raider on him. Henry started shouting for David to shoot the dog, shoot the dog. There was no way I was gonna let that happen. I had my gun out, and when Dave brought his up to shoot my buddy here"—I ran my hands through the dog's fur— "I tried firing toward his shoulder. Jess jumped, and my shot took her through both cheeks. I collapsed as I watched both of them fall. I think I passed out or hit my head again at that point." I was trying not to sob, but it was difficult.

"And why would David go along with what Henry was saying, about keeping you here prisoner and shooting your dog?" Grandpa asked, a hint of anger leaching into his voice.

"It has to do with the blackmail, doesn't it?" Grandma asked.

I nodded. "Jess' father and mother found this old phone bunker that'd been abandoned. They were part of the group, but they claimed it for their own as other people had been building and setting up their own shelters. Henry had them convinced that others were jealous, and they really had more room here than they needed. They didn't wanna be kicked out of their fall-back location. I don't even know what it's like in town, so I can imagine what the thought of being exiled would be like for them. I mean, all their stuff is here, their food, everything."

"Well, town is a place to be avoided right now. There's a whole bunch of ne'er-do-wells that came roaring in yesterday. Couple days back I fired up the tractor and moved the coop after making sure we had enough food for a while. Good thing we did it when we did, because things inside were starting to get bare again. If we'd waited just one more day to do that, they'd likely have heard the tractor."

"They would've heard your grandpa cussing when Foghorn lit into him." Grandma's words were funny, but she had a serious expression on her face.

"I heard there were a bunch of people who were gonna be joining the Hillbilly Mafia. Bunch of hard cases, is that what these guys look like?" I asked them.

"They definitely didn't take too well when they heard us driving. Couple of them like to have chased us down, but Grandma made them stop."

"What do you mean? What happened?"

Grandma looked at me and grinned, her teeth

showing. "I rode shotgun. Literally." She let out a chuckle. "I dusted a couple of their vehicles with buckshot, and they backed off. Then your grandpa drove like a hellion, and here we are."

Carter grunted, a smile touching his lips. He'd been silent but watchful, staring at the little girl whose hair shone in a halo around her tiny head. I heard footsteps and looked toward the staircase; Emily was coming down the stairs, her face a mask of rage. I shuddered, having seen before what she could do when she lost control. She saw me sitting by Mary and started taking the steps two at time. At some point Raider had laid across my legs, but when he heard her coming, he stood. A low grumble came from deep in his chest, and I knew what he was thinking. Was she a threat? Many of the people he thought of as his friends had turned out not to be. I pulled him back to my chest and spoke softly, pushing his guard hairs down and stroking the fur along his back.

"Thank you for watching Mary," Emily said, walking up to us, looking to my grandparents and then back to me.

"Emily, this is my grandpa and grandma, they came here to bust me out."

"Nice to meet you, Miss Emily," Grandpa said, looking between me and the young woman and back.

"Right now, may not be the right time, but you and I got to talk," Emily said, stopping in front of me.

Raider went rigid with the tone of her voice and let out an open-mouth growl.

"Don't you be getting lippy with me too," Emily said, pointing at Raider, and then walked over and roughly pet his head. "My nerves are shot, so don't take it out on me. I can't help it."

Her words were punctuated by how fast she pet the dog. He relaxed slightly, but he was still standing between me and her.

"Did you get him buried?" I asked her.

Grandpa shot me a puzzled look, but I ignored him.

"Jess and her mom are out there filling in the hole. Duke and Jimmy are out there, but there's a big group of... Well, the rest of the survival group here. They're on their way in right now. I don't know what's going on, but Henry and some of his buddies are leading."

"You mean they let him loose?" I asked her, feeling alarmed.

I didn't know where my gun was. After I'd shot David in the face somebody must've kicked it away from me and picked it up. Grandpa heard the tone of my voice, probably the anxiety, and reached into the right pocket of his well-worn bib and partially pulled out a small snub-nosed revolver. He went to put it back in after showing me, but I held my hand out.

"Let me have that, Grandpa," I said softly as I pushed Raider out of my way gently and stood. "I'll be the last person they'd expect to have a gun again. Just in case things get dicey."

Grandpa handed it over, and I saw that it was an old H&R five shot hammerless .38 Smith & Wesson.

This one actually broke open from the top, the catch being right by the top sight. I opened it and checked all five chambers were full. I closed it and put it in my pocket just as Grandma opened her purse.

"Do you want mine too?" Grandma asked, showing me she had one as well.

I knew Grandpa had this old gun from back when I was a kid, but I hadn't seen it in a long, long time. Having two of them, and Grandma having one in her purse? What were they expecting when they got here? I wondered what had tripped their spidey senses.

"Hey, baby girl, how are you feeling?" Emily knelt, brushing her daughter's hair back out of her face.

Mary's eyes were open again, and she reached for her mom's hand. She took it in both of hers tenderly.

"Mama, where can we go now?"

She'd woken up at some point, and I had no idea how much she'd heard. My back had been turned to her until Emily had moved. I guessed she'd heard quite a bit.

"We're going to stay right here for now, baby," she said, pulling her hand free and then rubbing Diesel's back. "That man who tried to hurt us is upstairs."

I cringed at her choice of words.

"But he's not coming down here, is he?" Mary asked quietly.

"Apparently they're going to have one of their versions of a town hall upstairs. I came back in as soon as I heard them to tell you that Jess and Linda will be in shortly."

"What do we need to do to get ready?" Grandpa asked me.

"I honestly don't know what to do," I told him, my head swimming a little bit.

I figured it was more the blood loss than the alcohol, and I kicked myself for having a drink, but I'd thought things were getting better. Henry should still be locked up and David buried. I wracked my brain, and then an idea clicked.

"You guys stay right here," I told them. "Grandma, don't let none of them fools touch Mary unless Duke or Carter say it's okay."

"What are you going to do?" Emily asked me suddenly.

"I'm going to see if they left any of the supplies in the room where they worked on us."

THE BACK ROOM WHERE THEY'D DONE THE MEATBALL surgery, and where Jess and Mary had been, was cleaned up pretty good. I could smell the bite of bleach water, and I looked under the counter and saw some of the same supplies I'd been using before. I grabbed a large container of ammonia and a gallon jug of bleach that felt half-full and, almost as an afterthought, some drain cleaner. I didn't see any of the chloroform that I'd made for them, and I assumed that they'd taken all the medical supplies out of here and stored them for next time.

As I was walking back, I stopped in the small storage closet that had been my room while I'd been healing up. I grabbed my backpack and dumped it out on the cot. I searched through all the clothing and miscellaneous stuff and found my pocket knife on the bottom, in my jeans. Then I loaded everything back in there, including the chemicals. At some point someone had left a couple of juice boxes in there, probably for Mary, but it might as well have been for me too. Didn't they tell you to drink juice after giving blood? With no way to really measure how much blood I'd given, I grabbed both, tossing one in my backpack before putting it over my shoulders.

As I was walking to the living room area that had been created in the large space, I could hear voices. At first, I figured it was just Grandpa, Grandma, Emily and Mary talking, but I heard a man say something in a sharp tone, and it wasn't my grandpa or Carter. I stuck the straw in the juice box and sucked it down as fast as I could with my left hand, while my right hand went to my pocket. I had been beaten up, shot, and had given as much blood as it took to help Miss Mary, and here I was thinking I was about to get into another fight. They say the definition of insanity is doing the same thing over and over but looking for a different result...

Call me crazy, but I wasn't going to stay trapped here, especially with Henry back in the picture.

5

DUKE, Carter, Jimmy, Jessica and Linda had joined everyone at the couches. Linda was sitting as far away from Mary and my grandparents as possible. I looked at her and she looked away, her face drawn. Jess was sitting closer to her, Yaeger next to her. My Raider buddy was sitting at little Mary's feet. The rest of the guys were all standing nearby. I could almost cut the tension in the air it was so thick. I looked between everyone to see what they were doing and talking about.

"Westley," Duke's voice was soft, "Henry and the rest of the mutual assistance group are meeting right now. All of us, including Linda and Jessica, have to go upstairs."

"Who let Henry out?" My voice was short and angry. "And why the hell is he here?"

"What are we gonna do?" Jimmy asked. "We can't hold him forever. We don't have that kind of manpower. We sent him back to his cabin and told him to stay there. Apparently, he went and rounded up everyone who was friendly with them." Jimmy's voice was much like mine, and I remembered he hadn't exactly been on my side when I'd woken up. Duke and Carter were both looking at him, with Linda, Jessica, and my grandparents staring at me.

"What are these town hall meetings?" Emily asked softly.

"It's where we all get together and decide on things for the group," Linda said. "At some point we were going to have to talk about what Henry had done. I thought the rest of the group already had a town hall meeting to talk about you working off your debts." Her words were quiet and soft, but her gaze was shooting daggers at me. "And now it looks like we're going to have to talk about what you have done."

I didn't say anything to that, what could I say?

"Linda, Jessica," a voice called from above.

"You and I are not finished," Linda said, pointing at me. "Don't go anywhere." Her voice cracked at the end, and a tear ran down the side of her face.

Jess looked stricken as she glanced at her mom, then up the stairs, pulling at her. She didn't spend a moment looking at me.

"Diesel, Yaeger," Jess called.

Mary moved so she wasn't laying directly on the dog, and the whole couch shifted when Diesel pushed off in a jump. Raider whined and started to follow, but I called him back.

"Stay," I said, patting him on the head.

He rewarded me with a lick on the hand. The rest of the MAG group (mutual assistance group) headed upstairs. Duke and Carter gave me a look I had no idea on how to interpret, but Jimmy ignored me as they headed upstairs. Emily was brushing little Mary's hair, and I sat across from them with my grandparents.

"So what's the plan?" Grandma asked me when she was sure we were not being overheard.

"I've got some ammonia and bleach," I said, pulling my pack in front of me and opening it up. "I figure there are two ways out of here, and Emily might be the only one healthy enough to go out that one. The second is upstairs, right through the group."

"That's where your chemistry skills come in?" Emily asked.

"What's hamestry?" Mary asked in a pained squeak.

"Shhh, honey, you shouldn't talk. Don't want to make the inside of your throat bleed."

"It's me mixing chemicals together to make something else. I don't think we should go today, though."

"Why the hell not?" Grandpa asked, and Emily nodded.

"Because Mary just got her neck sewn shut, and if we move her too fast..." I let the words trail off; only Emily could appreciate how much blood had come out of her daughter as I was knocked out.

"Oh dear," Grandma said softly, getting up and

moving to the couch, sitting on the other side of the little girl.

"But if this Henry fella is as bad a dude as you say he is, what's to stop him having you ... um..." Grandpa's words trailed off, but the missing word was *shot*.

"He originally wanted to keep me around because I know how to make useful things for them. I don't know what he's after now. I know Raider here chewed on him something good."

Raider let out a chuffing sound.

"I'm not going to be held prisoner here any longer, but I can't leave Emily and Mary behind. I've got to stay, if only a little longer."

Voices rose into a yelling match from somewhere upstairs. It was faint to my ears, but we all turned to stare. I couldn't make out the words. I wished I had Raider's hearing right about now. More shouting followed, and then heavy footsteps could be heard coming down the stairs at a run.

"Something's going on, something's happening," Grandpa said, reaching for his pocket, only to stop when he remembered I had gotten the pistol from him.

Duke burst into sight, taking the stairs three at a time, his face a rictus of surprise.

"You must hurry," he said, sweat beading his brow.

He was pointing toward the back of the shelter. Everyone got up but me; I had my hands in my dog's fur, listening to above.

"Westley Flagg," he said in a deep voice that

snapped me out of my thoughts, then he made a hurry gesture.

I started to get up while putting on my backpack, but gunfire erupted above and seemingly all around us. My eyes went wide, but I was moving already. I was going to scoop Mary up, but Emily had already gotten to her. Raider ran ahead as the rest of us caught up with Duke.

"What's going on?" I asked, feeling a little bit dizzy, foolish, and panicked.

"We're being attacked," Duke said, turning.

The long hallway leading to the room the surgery had been performed in seemed a mile long. We stopped in front of a door, just a room away from the closet my grandma had found me in. Duke fished for keys and put one in, turning it. It opened into a small room, the mechanical room by the looks of things. A water heater and what looked like a hodgepodge boiler system were the only things in it. I looked at Duke skeptically.

"There's an air duct in the back to vent the room. The screen is held on with tension clips. Jessica set this up and only told me about it. You have to get everyone about twenty feet down the venting and out of sight."

A scream echoed above us, and automatic gunfire startled everyone. It sounded close. Way too close.

"Are we—" Emily started to say.

"I don't know," Duke told her. "Now *git*."

I got ahead of everyone and took my pack off. I found the vent cover he was talking about and pulled it loose. It looked like an oversized cold air return. The direction seemingly pointed straight into the mountain. The galvanized metal had been here a long, long time. I felt like I needed a tetanus shot just from looking at it.

"Mommy, I don't wanna go in there," Mary said softly, crying.

Duke smacked his forehead and pulled out a small prescription bottle and handed it to Emily. I fished in my backpack and found the flashlight I always kept in the pouch with my spare compass and map. I handed it to Emily, and she put Mary down and gave her the light. Mary crawled in the hole, crying as somebody else above screamed, but it sounded more like an agonized wail. That, more than anything else, got the little girl moving.

Emily followed her, and I motioned for Grandma and Grandpa to go next.

"I'd rather stand and—"

"Move yer wrinkled old ass before I stick my foot up it," Grandma growled in a voice that sounded close to Duke's conversational tone. Deep.

Grandpa was about to go, but Raider darted ahead, to catch up with the ladies. Grandpa made an after you motion, bowing, before following the dog.

"If you fart, Furface, I'm going to ... stop, that's my ... shit," Grandpa muttered as I heard something metallic hit as Grandma was on all fours to follow him. "Dropped my flask."

"I'll drop your ass if you don't hurry," Grandma said, her voice coming out in gasps.

"I need to go, Jess said to get you guys safe."

"Is she ok?" I asked him as Grandma's feet disappeared.

"I don't know. Henry didn't just bring his followers from the group, he brought—"

Gunfire echoed, and he staggered back. He drew a pistol and started firing. I wasn't sure if he'd been hit or not, but I saw him work the lock with his left hand and pull the door closed behind him, his gun hardly letting up. It was black in here, and I hesitated too long. Go help him? Go with my family? I heard Raider bark softly, and I knew what I had to do. I backed into the shaft feet first and felt in the darkness until I found the gate. Somebody had fashioned a handle for the back side with what felt like soldered on wire. I moved it around and then felt it click into place.

More gunfire, more shouts. What did he mean? Henry didn't come alone with just his followers? Then who were they? I was starting to feel like there were no good guys in this game. Not even me. I'd killed my girlfriend's father so he wouldn't kill my dog. I'd been betrayed by her family, her group. They'd lied to me about ... well, about almost everything, and now I was on the run again. But from whom?

I struggled, but I was able to turn around in the cramped space, and I crawled into the darkness, a pinpoint of light to lead my way.

6

WE FOUND ourselves at the junction that Duke had told me about. I dug in my backpack and found a short stubby candle, one I'd kept around for soft light while reading or looking something up. I held my hand out for the flashlight from Mary, but the little girl shook her head. I didn't argue, just pushed my backpack in front of the shaft's opening and looked at where we were while I fished for a lighter.

The round galvanized pipe that had brought us here led to a small concrete room, barely six feet by six feet, and only about four feet tall. There were two other pipes on the level going off in other directions, one across from us and one to my left. There was one that opened above, and from that I could smell more than feel fresh air coming in. On one side there were two old wooden produce crates, a bucket, and two cases of water.

"Cozy accommodations, isn't it?" Grandpa asked, only to get a smack on the back of the head.

That made him jerk his head to the side, and he got the wall, letting out a surprised yelp. Mary started giggling, and Emily looked at me, grinning. The gunfire had slacked off; it wasn't so booming and deafening now. I fished for the lighter and found it in my backpack. I lit the small candle and put it off to the side, so it wasn't directly shining light down the shaft we'd just been in, then held my hand out for the flashlight again. This time, Mary gave it to me, but you could tell she was reluctant. I snapped it off and put it in my backpack again and called Raider over to me with a gesture.

He snorted, turned around in a circle, and sat across Mary's legs.

"Traitor," I muttered and found a spot in the cramped quarters next to Grandma.

"What is this place?" she whispered.

"Kind of like a plenum in a furnace," I whispered back. "Probably leads to other parts of the area. Probably to vent fumes from the old generators and to bring in fresh air."

"Vent fumes?" Grandpa asked, surprise in his voice.

"I'm guessing here, but since Jessica stocked this place up, I doubt it's dangerous to us," I whispered, trying to keep my voice down.

I could hear a banging sound from far off, then I realized it was somebody knocking on the utility room door, and I was hearing it echo from the shaft opening.

I held my hand up for everyone to be quiet then picked up the candle in case I had to blow it out quickly. More pounding. Raider let out a whine and got to his feet, his ears brushing the low ceiling, and stood in front of the ladies. Grandma reached into her purse, but she just kept her hand there and didn't pull anything out. I knew what she was doing; she had a hand on her little .38.

Emily pushed Raider to the side so she could see me and made a head bob toward the vent shaft on the left, then shrugged her shoulders as if, what do you think? I shrugged and made a stay here motion, then handed the candle to Grandpa and got on my stomach. I belly crawled ten, then twenty feet into the vent shaft, toward the room we'd just fled from, and waited. I could almost make out voices. Then I realized I could, two of them, and I recognized who was speaking.

"...I don't care what you do with that big bastard. If you don't kill him, I will. I want Wes and the brat found. I don't care about the rest. Kill them all." Henry's words were almost a scream.

My blood went cold. I'd heard that tone from him before, when he'd been losing his cool and getting chewed on by my dog.

"...thinks up the shaft, the way we had to lower him down when he was knocked out. The rope..." I missed the words as a string of gunfire and curses above cut his words off or made it so I couldn't hear anymore.

I heard something behind me and was turning as a big, hairy lug flopped down on my back. My pup had come back, and with nowhere to sit beside me, he'd sat on me.

"Raider," I said turning, trying to be quiet, pushing at him.

He got up and, as he backed up, two of four paws hit me in the nads. I tried not to barf and pulled my knees to my stomach, taking deep breaths. I heard the dog chuff from behind me, but he wasn't loud, and I was listening to the sudden silence again.

"...he's dead," a voice I didn't recognize said.

I hoped it was Henry, I hoped so hard my nausea seemingly went away. That or Jimmy. Jimmy was talking with Henry? Working with him? Good information to have known instead of suspected.

"Too bad, his medical skills would have been great, since the doc was killed," Henry's voice answered.

I mentally cursed. May the fleas of a thousand camels infest his sack. I was about to go on when I heard another agonized scream.

"...and kill that bitch," Henry said.

I shivered. Where was Jessica? Who was he talking about?

The voices rose and fell, and I felt Raider slowly moving across me again, up my legs until his big head was resting on the small of my back. I folded my arms and lay my head on them as I listened. I sat like that for a long time. Somewhere behind me the candle was blown out. I was in total, absolute darkness. If I crawled far enough forward, I could probably see light coming from the crack under the door in the utility room, but I now knew what people meant when they said it was as dark as sin.

The corrugated metal was cold, musty, and rusty smelling, but Raider was giving me some of his warmth. I struggled to stay sharp, to listen. Above me and ahead of me, I could hear things, as if somebody was moving heavy things around. I got sleepy. When things quieted down, I found Raider had fallen asleep on my back. I wiggled enough that he awoke with a snort, then started backing up. I followed him until we were in the small junction area. The candle had been lit again, and I had no idea how much time had passed. Everyone was sleeping. Grandma had her arms crossed, and Grandpa was snoring softly, his flask in his hand, the cap still on tight.

Emily had Mary on her lap, the little girl's head resting against her mother's chest. She'd fallen sideways and was leaned between the wall and the cases of water to prop up her right side. The little girl was snoring softly. I could see the prescription bottle. It didn't have a pharmacist's label on it, but it did have felt tipped marker written on it. It had smudged, but I saw enough letters to make out it was amoxicillin and in a light dose. Perfect for a kid. Duke had come through at the last second, probably realizing that without these antibiotics, her chances of infection would go through the roof.

As gently as I could, I snaked a bottle of water out of the case and looked in the wooden crate. Pouches of Mountain House and Prego Ready-meals were stashed inside the one I peeked into. There was a Ziplock bag of forks and spoons on the side, and I got one of each out and grabbed a Ready-meal and sat back with my feast. I sipped on water and ate some sort of pasta and sausage dish right out of the pouch. I propped my back against the crates while I ate and tried to get a coherent thought to go through my head, but failed.

Too much, too fast. I'd gone from being hurt, to willingly bled dry, to save the little girl. My body needed food and water as much as it needed rest. Maybe after I slept, I could think more clearly. I had to go topside and check on Jess. I put my stuff to the side, and Raider whined, smelling the pouch. I'd get him one of his own when I woke up. I was tired, and it would take too much energy to do that now. I sat the pouch up and poured half my water into it and pushed it on the floor to him.

I heard a little sound and saw Mary had woke up and was looking around. She was starting to fuss. I reached my hand over and touched her arm. She turned to see me and smiled. She crawled out of her mom's lap, into mine, and curled up sideways so she could see everyone in the room. Raider let out a chuff and sat next to us, before stretching and putting his back against me and the little girl. Her weight was comforting. I could smell the topical medication they had used on her neck. Sleep. I needed sleep. I'd been underground so long I didn't even know what time of day it was.

I woke as somebody was gently pulling Mary out of my arms. Raider?! He'd be going crazy if it was somebody he didn't know. Why was it so dark in here? A match flared up as Grandpa lit the candle. I saw it was Grandma who'd pulled Mary from me and settled her into her lap.

"You've done so much, you get some good rest. Let me cuddle this little one."

I stretched out, feeling my tendons pop, and nodded then listened. Silence. I could smell something, though, wood smoke? Fire? I looked over and saw Emily was still out cold. I went under the vertical shaft and stood and stretched, feeling my shoulder burn as I put my hands over my head. I rolled it experimentally and was rewarded with shooting bolts of pain. I'd have to work on keeping it stretched out for a while, or my arm was likely to be useless.

"You get you some rest," Grandma repeated.

"I've got to find out what's going on," I told her, watching Grandpa raise the flask to his lips and take a sip.

"We don't know what's going on. It's best to stay put until we do know," she said as if that was the final word.

"Only way we're going to know what's going on is if one of us goes up and looks. Besides, I'm going to check out these side shafts to see if they lead anywhere useful. If we can't come back the way we came in..."

"What do you mean?" Grandpa asked.

"I'm pretty sure Duke was shot getting the door closed. The keys ... they're inside the room there, but if they really wanted to, they could bust in or blow the door. I don't think this spot is safe for long. I need to find us a way out."

"I'm coming with you," Grandpa said softly.

"No, I need you to stay here and help Grandma with Mary and Emily. Raider, you too," I said, noting the dog had followed Grandma and was sitting near the girl.

He seemed to have an instinct about knowing where he was needed and when. I was a bit jealous, but now wasn't the time; besides, I had a feeling I wouldn't be able to use his help crawling through the vent shafts. I looked up into the darkness above me, then got down and got my flashlight out of my pack. I used one hand to cup the front of it and pointed it up and clicked it on. I saw the same corrugated steel pipe heading straight up ninety degrees from the ground. I un-cupped the light and let the bright LEDs illuminate. It went further than I could make out, with one side opening that looked about fifty feet straight up in the air.

"Go check out the side."

"Are you taking a flashlight with you?" Grandpa asked, looking at the dwindling candle.

"I've got another candle in my backpack," I told him softly. Emily twitched in her sleep, and Mary was snoring softly.

. . .

GRANDMA SMOOTHED HER HAIR BACK. SHE MADE A SOFT sound and settled down. She looked like she was dreaming, and nobody wanted to wake her.

"What's your story there?" Grandma said, looking over Mary's small head.

"She's the granddaughter," I said, confused why she would ask.

"That's not what I'm talking about, Westley," Grandma said softly. "You know what I'm talking about."

Yes, I did, but this wasn't the time nor place.

"Raider, you stay here with Grandma and Grandpa, got it?"

Raider chuffed, and then laid his head on his paws.

I MOVED THROUGH THE TUNNEL AS QUIETLY AS I COULD, learning quickly that if I moved too fast, I would make it echo. Since I didn't know who had attacked us, other than that they were tied to Henry, nor how many there were, I figured being quiet was prudent. The tunnel seemed to go for sixty feet, and then turn gently to the right. I used the flashlight intermittently, letting it shine through my fingers for short bursts. Since I didn't have any night vision in absolute darkness anyway, I dealt with the after images of having the light turn on and off. I didn't want to take a chance of my light giving away our position and hiding place.

There was another curve to the right again, and I suddenly realized that it was possible that both of these tunnels that came from the junction room were connected. At this point I wasn't worried about getting lost, because all I had to do was go back the way I came. But I would have to make some choices if I came to some sort of intersection. As I crawled around the next corner, I saw that the galvanized pipe had collapsed. Small pebbles and sand littered the floor where it looked like a giant weight had simply crushed the metal pipe together.

It made my blood run cold; if this had happened naturally, could it have happened elsewhere too? It was tight quarters once again, but with my shoulder protesting, I was able to get myself contorted and turned around. Going back was easier than I had thought, and with no outlets into other portions of the underground facility, I was able to go faster. When I got back into the junction, I saw that everyone had fallen asleep once more. There were food wrappers next to Grandpa's sleeping form. Raider was laying between Grandpa and Grandma's legs, with little Mary's hand on top of his head. He looked at me, licked his lips, and then closed his eyes again. The candle was getting low, but I guessed it had a couple hours left on it still.

I took it easy and went into the other opening, knowing I couldn't crawl my way up the vertical shaft with my shoulder and arm the way it was. Right away, I knew this ventilation shaft was different. It seemed to be newer and had a sharp ninety degree turn within twenty feet of the junction room. I made the turn and laid on my side and flicked on the flashlight. It opened into what looked like another junction room. Curious, I crawled in and then took my left hand off the flashlight and looked around.

The room was much the same as the junction room where everyone was sleeping. The difference was it looked empty, with no exits, but there was a ladder made from rusty rebar built into the left wall, almost hidden. If I hadn't walked in and looked behind me, I would've missed it and the vertical shaft above it. I got under the opening and stood, stretching my aching leg muscles. My shoulder was starting to bug me from crawling around on all fours, and I spent a moment stretching it. I flashed the light up and saw that it traveled about twenty feet and then seemed to turn off on a forty-five-degree angle. At least that was what it looked like from where I was standing.

I didn't want to climb up; something about it filled me with dread. The rusty rebar, the distance, the visions of me falling, screaming, and getting hurt, or worse—leaving everyone to take care of me, or bury me somewhere in the darkness. I shook my head. I'd been having a lot of morbid thoughts lately and they weren't productive. I needed to think about happy times, times when I was having fun even when I knew things could go sideways. Things like running a big load of moonshine, the feeling of satisfaction of me and Raider taking on Lance's bully boys at the back of the honky-tonk. Kissing Jessica in the moonlight.

Jessica.

"Ain't no rest for the wicked," I muttered to myself, and started climbing.

I made it to where the shaft turned off, a forty-five-degree angle and not another sideways shaft where I could crawl normally. This still had rungs on it, and unlike the lower portions, these weren't covered in scales of rust and corrosion. The air here smelled funny, though. Almost like a chemical smell. I turned the flashlight on for a second and then immediately snapped it off. I could see that thirty or forty rungs of the ladder ahead of me was another grate.

As quietly as I could, I climbed. I had snapped the flashlight off, but now I stored it in my back pocket. It wouldn't do to sit on, but it got it out of my way. A sudden screeching noise had me almost jump right out of my skin. It was metal on metal, and for half a second, I thought it was coming from below me. I worried that the tube I was in was at risk of collapsing, like I'd found in the other side of the ventilation shafts down below. Then I heard voices, and they were coming from the other side of the grate, not above or behind me.

"I swear Jimmy, if you don't let me go right now, I'm gonna cut your throat in your sleep. You double-crossing son of a bitch!" Jessica's voice rang out ahead of me.

I heard a slapping sound, unmistakable. Flesh against flesh, and Jess let out a groan. I heard a zipping sound and what sounded like a struggle ahead of me.

"I don't want to have to do this, but if you keep fighting me on this, I'll hit you again. Hold still, I'm just going to tie you up here until Henry tells me what we're doing."

"You hit me again... You're gonna regret it." There was something cold in Jess' voice, and I knew what that tone meant.

She'd made the decision, and if she got her chance, she was going to bury Jimmy. I heard another zipping sound and then another screech of metal on metal. Light flashed from the cover in front of me, and I pushed myself back, hoping that my face wasn't being lit up on the other side of the slats. I could see that there was something directly in front of the vent a couple inches away, but I didn't know what it was. Then the screeching noise again, and then silence. Darkness.

In the gloom, I heard Jessica start crying. I'd love to say that I ran right out and saved her, but I waited a good five minutes, listening to her crying and mumbling softly. Half of it was threats and curses, half of it was her mumbling her father's name, and her mother's, over and over. Sporadic gunfire could be heard, but nothing like it had been before. The more important thing was none of it seemed to be very close. Gathering my courage, I put my fingers on the grate and started pushing slowly.

The grate popped forward, and I realized it was on tension clips, just like the one downstairs. I pushed it to the side, and Jessica suddenly quit crying and sobbing.

"Who's there?" Jessica said softly.

I couldn't see anything, it was dark, and I didn't want to risk using the flashlight just yet. I softly pushed on what looked like a wooden chest that'd been stacked in front of the grate. It rolled a lot easier than I'd expected, and I almost fell forward and overcompensated. I grabbed the rung before I could go backward and then climbed in the darkness.

I got to my feet on what sounded like wood flooring and snapped on my flashlight. Jessica turned her head away from the harsh light of my LEDs, and I got a quick glimpse. Her legs had been zip tied together, her arms behind her, with her hands around the support beam of a small room, roughly twelve by twelve. I could see the plastic biting into her flesh. Two walls were made from concrete block, a third looked like it was stone that had been blasted right into the side of the mountain. The last wall was metal, the kind you would use in pole barns. Metal cupboards lined two of the walls, and three pallets and a wooden trunk had been blocking the air grate.

"Jessica, are you okay?" I asked, pointing the flashlight straight at the ground so I wouldn't blind her.

Jessica looked over at me sharply, her eyes growing wide as she saw me. Her lip had a cut on it, which was half swollen closed. She had blood splatter on the side of her face, and I could see some of the stitches in her mouth had ripped loose. She spit blood off to the side and then looked up at me again with bloodstained teeth.

"I think I am now. Cut me loose."

7

I EASILY GOT Jessica loose using my pocketknife. She immediately went to the trunk that I had pushed and felt under it, then let out a strange sound as she ripped a piece of tape off the bottom. She held up a key ring and immediately went to one of the metal cupboards. She unlocked it and pulled the door open, then moved to the one on her left and unlocked and opened the second one.

I immediately realized what this little place was. Right off the bat in the right locker I saw the M4 I'd taken off the man I'd killed, along with Grandpa's silenced bolt gun, and dozens of other weapons. I looked at the pallets and then to Jessica. I realized this was the armory. Where were we exactly? They must've been pretty sure they had Jessica subdued and patted down, because they'd locked her in a building full of weapons. Weapons she knew how to use very well.

"Thank you," she said after a moment.

I heard her pulling back the slide on a carbine, which I would swear was the same one I'd seen her carrying before. She put a stiff belt around her waist that had the holster on the right side and pouches that slid around the belt. She adjusted them and put them to where one was over her right pocket with the other on her left hip. I picked up the silenced rifle and set it aside and then picked up the M4 I'd taken off the man I'd killed.

"Did everyone make it into the fallback spot?" Jessica asked before I had a chance to answer her thanks.

"Yeah, I got Grandpa, Grandma, Emily and Mary into that transition area. Sorry we got into your food a bit."

"This is bad, Wes, this is really bad. The guys that we've been getting reports on? The druggies that had hooked up with Lance and had taken over his group? That's who Henry is with."

I understood her words and I nodded, but I was privately blown away as it really was a case of not knowing who to trust.

"Do you have a plan?" I asked her quietly.

"If everyone is safe for now, we need to see what's going on here, and see if it's safe to escape."

I nodded in agreement and started loading the hush puppy. I hadn't brought my backpack with me, but I saw a belt similar to Jessica's in the middle locker. I reached over and pulled it to me and adjusted it and snapped it on. It had a funny catch in the front, and the belt itself seemed like it was made from a rigid piece of plastic. It had no sag in it the way my leather belt did when I was wearing my gun under my shirt, but it was equipped with what I realized were dump pouches. Then I reached up and took a 1911 and three magazines off the top shelf, then stood back so Jessica could do the same.

I had limited ammunition for the hush puppy, but there were loaded AR magazines in the bottom of both metal cabinets. I looked at the side of the receiver of the M4 and made sure it was on no pew, before inserting a magazine and pulling the charging handle. One click up would be pew, and one more click all the way back to me would be pew, pew, pew. I tried not to be amused at that, and I started stuffing the dump pouches with magazines.

"Where are your dogs?" I asked her.

"Yaeger and Diesel tried to run off with my mom, but Diesel..." her words trailed off, and she wiped a tear from her eye. "Henry's going to pay."

I filled the pouch. I lost count of how many loaded magazines I packed in. Enough to kill everyone ten times over at least.

"You got too many mags, you're gonna rattle," Jessica said.

I nodded and went over to the wooden chest. I put the grate in after setting the guns down, and then pushed the chest into place covering up the ventilation shaft behind it. Then I unloaded the dump pouch and took my shirt off. I wished I had my backpack with me.

I would use an extra pair of socks for this, but I didn't, so I had to make do with what I had. Jessica was about to say something, probably questioning what I was doing when I pulled my knife out and started cutting strips off the bottom of my shirt.

I started putting the magazines in the dump pouches, weaving the strips of cotton cloth between them until I had it full. I only ended up putting two magazines on the bottom of the cabinet by the time I was done, but Jessica was grinning slightly. I could tell it hurt her mouth to do so, and there was a trickle of blood coming down the side of her cheek from where the stitches had torn out.

"What?" I asked.

"Is that a new style, Mr. Flagg?" she asked, looking at my stomach. I looked down and saw that three inches above the belt was bare from where I had torn the bottom of my shirt off.

"Didn't you know? Things are different nowadays, guys can wear belly shirts too."

I said it with a straight face, but I couldn't help the snort that came out. Jessica rolled her eyes at me and then locked up the cabinets. Then she walked to the steel door that was set into the metal wall of the enclosure. I picked up my flashlight and shined it at her feet so she would get the back wash of light and not be blinded, and she used that to fish out a brass-colored key. She put it in the deadbolt and turned it. The lock opened with a *snick.*

"How many of them are out there?" I asked, trying

to decide if I wanted to carry both rifles or just one.

"It seemed like a couple hundred to me, but it was probably no more than an extra thirty or forty people. Henry had apparently recruited about half of our MAG group, but the half that he didn't were either shot or they fled when the fighting started. We weren't expecting a double cross like this."

"How long has it been since the attack?"

"It's been about four hours. They caught me and my mom flat-footed, but she punched Henry as she ran. They kept me under guard until Jimmy came for me just a little while ago. I think they're hoping they can use me to get my mom to come out of hiding."

"I know this isn't the time, but I thought you were the one they really had to worry about?"

Jessica had her hand on the door, ready to open it. "In some ways. But it's my mom who really scares them. She wasn't always Miss Susie Homemaker. I don't even know what she used to do before she married my dad."

My jaw dropped open at that; I knew her mom was a bad ass, and that people deferred to her. I'd kind of blown that off when I'd seen the way Henry had taken things over when I'd been hurt. I'd had no idea, I'd just thought she was good at what she did. I remembered how everyone referred to her for things, until Henry was around. Then she seemed really quiet and submissive. I couldn't follow that train of thought for long, because Jessica was starting to open the door and peek out.

"Do you know how to do more than just shoot?" Jessica asked me.

"I'm pretty handy at making things go boom, as long as I've got the right materials," I told her.

"How familiar are you with grenades and claymores?"

"Why, you got some of those laying around?"

She grinned, despite the blood trickling down either side of her face.

ONCE WE WERE OUTSIDE OF THE BUILDING, I SAW IT WAS nothing more than a metal facing recessed into the rock on a large slope somewhere near where they had lowered me in. I hadn't seen this when I was being carried in the first time, but I'd been in and out of things.

"Remember, face it outward," Jessica said as I set the claymore down in the gap the door had made.

I USED A PIECE OF DUCT TAPE ON THE BOTTOM EDGE OF the door to some black wire Jessica had gotten out of the third steel cabinet, along with some other goodies and a handy dandy black, nondescript backpack. It sat uncomfortably on my shoulders, but I planned on making it lighter. Finally, I hooked the wire to the claymore and pushed the door against it. I finished it off with breaking off a small stick and wedging it in front of the door. That way the wind hopefully wouldn't be able to tear the door open, which would set off the charge prematurely. When that was done, Jessica nodded at me, then she motioned with her head and we headed into the brush, off the trail from the side of their mountain redoubt.

We could hear voices, shouts. It was hard to distinguish who was doing what, but I followed Jess, who was moving low in a hunched over manner. I was a bit larger than her and could only do half a crouch, but I kept the silenced rifle in front of me to push the brush away. It wasn't properly dark yet, but I could see it would be full on night soon. I wished I'd found the NVGs I'd taken off the guy at the Crater of Diamonds, but I'd managed just fine over the years while poaching. I didn't need much light to make out shapes and movement in the coming darkness.

"Most of the MAG group has their houses and cabins down in the bottom," Jessica said after ten minutes of walking. "I want to get close enough to make out what they're saying."

"Ok, but how do we know who's who?" I asked her.

"At this point, I think anybody walking around free is with Henry," she said, her voice low and quiet.

"Ok, which way—"

"Shhh," she said and made a motion I took to mean get down.

I dropped as quickly and quietly as I could. Within a minute, I could hear the voices, and they were getting louder. I tried to breathe low and shallow, not holding my breath. It was a mental exercise to keep my focus and to keep from getting tunnel vision, something Grandpa had taught me years ago. My heart was racing as I crawled next to Jessica, my rifle in front of me. I went stiff as I saw the brush about ten feet ahead of me move, far ahead of the voices. I recognized the form: it was Jimmy. He wasn't following the normal rabbit path that had led from the armory. He was going through the brush, the same way a poacher would. I gave the guy credit. I'd seen him in action before. He'd been there at the homestead when the guys on the four wheelers had come after Lester. Despite everything he'd done, he'd been a lying traitorous snake. For that, he was going to pay. I waited for him to take a step, then another. Then a third, but he stepped on a brittle branch that made a snap. I timed flicking the safety off as best as I could, but he stopped dead.

I waited, my gun more or less pointed between his shoulders as he turned, scanning the area, seemingly oblivious to his soon appointed time to die.

He lifted a walkie talkie to his lips. "Jessica is locked in the armory. No sign of Wes nor anyone else, over."

"Half your targets are either old, hurt, or too weak to have made that climb. Are you sure there's no other way out of the bunker? Over."

"Unless they're hiding really good and staying quiet, we couldn't find any sign of them Henry, over."

"Keep looking. Have the group I sent with you wait inside the armory in case they try to come spring

Jessica loose. There's only so many places to hide and I want to round them up, so we can get this operation underway again. Over."

Jimmy pulled the walkie talkie away from his lips and flipped it off with his left hand, then pulled it close. "Understood. Jimmy out."

He clipped the walkie talkie to his belt, then turned, scanning the bushes. I paused my breathing, hearing Jessica do the same as I willed us to be invisible, still. Our cover wasn't great, but it was getting dark out and probably nobody had been using any sort of light discipline. That was confirmed a moment later when Jimmy pulled a handgun and turned on the light under the barrel, then started moving away from us. I waited thirty seconds and then turned to look at Jess. Her rifle was up, and she had about three pounds of tension on a four-pound trigger. Her carbine was tracking him still, though he was nearly out of my sight. She saw me, and I held up a finger for her to wait, then pointed to the direction we'd come from. She nodded.

The voices that had been following soon materialized into shapes, then individual people, walking on the trail about twenty feet away from us. Three men and two women followed. I recognized half of them from the MAG group, but the other half looked right out of Soldier of Fortune magazine. They wore black BDUs, like the man I'd killed in the night raid, and were heavily armed.

I pointed to my suppressor on the rifle, then back

at the group, and held up a finger. I hoped she understood that I wanted to wait, but I'd use my rifle if needed so we didn't give away our position. Jess nodded after a moment, and we started to belly crawl back the way we'd come. I could hear the men and women talking quietly. Most were wondering about the whereabouts of me and the rest of us who had hid in the ventilation. I was surprised when I didn't hear Linda's name mentioned.

"Look, someone's been in here," a voice said.

"Cover me," Jimmy said quietly, and the rest seemed to stack up behind him.

We had a good view of things, but I realized that if we weren't careful and moved up too far, we'd be in the radius of all the ball bearings that were almost ready to tear life from—

BOOM

The world seemed to shake as the claymore went off. Jimmy and the first man who'd stacked up behind him were turned into bags of pink mist, and two others fell, slapping at their bodies. The noise was so loud I didn't hear the screams at first. One of the men in the back turned to start running. Jess tapped my shoulder, and I stood, tracking him with my scope in the fading light. I let my breath out slow and gently pulled the trigger, feeling the moment when there was no more resistance. A popping noise punctuated the screams, and I saw red erupt from the base of the man's skull. He dropped.

Jess moved forward, pushing the metal door closed

and locking it. Then I saw her pull her knife.

She kicked the dropped guns away from the bodies; some were still flopping around. I stepped forward, not wanting to watch, but unable to look away while she finished off several of them, leaving them to bleed. I saw something twitch and stepped forward. Jimmy had been blown nearly in half, but he was trying to lift what was left of his arm. A bubble of blood burst from his lips, and his eyes went wide when he saw me.

"A knife's too good for you," I told him quietly and stepped on his throat.

"Wes, no," Jessica urged, pulling on me.

I ground my boot as hard as I could before she nearly pulled me off my feet. He'd quit breathing, his eyes staring at nothing.

"They're going to be coming soon. We've got seconds, we need to move."

The stuff, the gear, the loot? I bent over to check on a fallen gun, but Jessica was pulling on me again. I followed her as she jogged down the trail. I knew we shouldn't be on the trail. As we were passing the man I'd shot, I called to her, "Wait."

I'd tugged at the small backpack he had on. It had a radio clipped to it, along with an earpiece and a PTT button on the front strap. Jessica was about to say something, when it came loose, and I pointed to the heavy brush. I followed her as she took off again. The radios of the dead men, including the one I was carrying, went off.

"Jimmy, Smith, do you copy?" Henry's voice came over the radio.

Jessica reached for it, but I held the pack away and put on the earpiece then keyed the mic, "Sorry, Henry, but Jimmy and Smith are unavailable at this time. Please leave your message after the boom."

"Who is... Westley?" he asked.

I was silent, waiting. I could hear more shouts and then somebody shot. Up slope, I heard the lead slap into something, a tree, the ground, I wasn't sure. Unless they had night sights, or night vision, they were just slinging lead randomly. I didn't want to give them anymore reason to home in on my location, so I kept my mouth shut.

Jessica tapped me, then pointed to the mic and made a 'go ahead' gesture.

"Hey, Henry, how many more of your friends want to end up dead?"

"Westley," his voice was a growl, "I'll kill every single member of your family, everyone you loved. You hear me?"

"If you could find them. Luckily for us, Grandpa knows how to hotwire an old truck. They should be miles away by now. Going for help. We hid out for hours waiting for you dumb shits to get complacent."

"We run this area! There's no help coming for you."

"I'm an old backwoods moonshiner from the hollers," I replied, trying not to raise my voice. "There's plenty of good ol' boys who'd throw their hat in the ring for me and Grandpa. I'm just here to buy them some time, jacking my jaw, wasting away the night..."

The feedback was mostly cursing while Henry screamed to somebody else to check the motor pool. He went on like that for a while, then must have realized he had the mic keyed.

"You know, if we had set this up better, we could have sabotaged the motor pool," Jessica whispered.

"Cutting throats, blowing people up. Great second date, huh?"

I meant that to be humorous, but her face wasn't smiling, and she wasn't amused.

"Listen, Jessica, about your father, I'm really—"

"Not right now," she said shortly, looking away. "I don't know if we can do anything more than die together. I don't want to have my last words to you be what I want to say at this moment."

I went silent, her words chilling me. I'd killed her father. I'd shot her in the face. In the heat of things, I hadn't let that go through my head, but I bet it was going through hers. She was right, though; by setting off that trap, our abilities of just sneaking and peeking were gone. They were going to hunt for us, unless they really thought we had fled. A germ of an idea was forming.

"What? You just had an idea," Jessica said as we moved deeper into the brush.

"Where's the last place they would expect us?" I asked her.

"In the bunker, but we can't set traps or have a

running gun battle down there. Too many chances for a rico…"

Ricochet. I knew what she was going to say, remembered Mary with her eyes closed, her throat neatly stitched up.

"Where's the second to the last place they would expect us?" I asked her.

"Henry's house," she said immediately.

"Now there's an idea."

"Are we going to get the rest out of there first?" she asked, her head tilted.

"What do you think of waiting and surprising the next group who comes around, looking for the guys we just killed?"

"I think it'd be a double trap. One for them, with more surrounding the area, looking for us to do the same and catch us in a crossfire, using their green troops for cannon fodder."

"Well, if they're going to set a trap around that area, how are we going to get into the bunker to get everyone out without them catching us?"

Jess held up a set of keys in the moonlight, then pocketed them again. "The way you went down the first time. I doubt they'll be looking there. First things first, though, we have to make a distraction."

"Now this I have to see," I said, feeling more than the heart and soul crushing pain from being too flippant, and trying to suppress the urge to apologize for what I had done to her father, for the fourth or fifth time.

8

I WAS glad I'd eaten and slept earlier. Full dark was always hard for me to stay awake, and even rested, it was a struggle. Jessica and I were sitting about a hundred yards from Henry's cabin, on a small rise covered in tall weeds and locust thorns. We had a good view down below, and it was scary. It looked like easily three dozen or more people had joined the small band of Henry's. He had been barking orders from the porch, but somebody had whispered something to him, and I could now hear him yelling out the front door of what looked like a log cabin.

I'd been eager to take a shot at him, but the angle was horrible, and the moon was to our backs. As long as we didn't move, we wouldn't be seen, but if we did something like start a fire, we'd not only have people all over us, but if we got up and ran, we'd be silhouetted. Not a good situation to be in when we were outnumbered twenty-five to one. Or more. Instead, we watched, whispering plans back and forth and listening to the chatter on the handhelds. For the most part, other than them, the forest was silent, and the smell of wood fires heating water and cooking food almost made everything feel normal.

It seemed that they thought there was a truck gone, after all. I grinned, knowing half the camp was about to go looking for it, leaving Henry and the others here alone. I worried about what my family was thinking, me gone, them alone without knowing what had happened, but if this worked out, we'd be out of here soon. Sooner than I had any right to be hopeful for.

"Now we wait," Jess whispered.

"Why don't we just burn them out?" I asked Jess, nodding to the wooden cabin below.

"It's got a fire-retardant finish. With the metal roof, only way to get it lit is to hit it with a rocket—"

"What about a Molotov?" I asked her, thinking of materials immediately.

"Wes, his cabin is hardened. It's fireproof, and bulletproof, except the windows, and he's got shutters that will stop most smaller calibers; with a metal roof, there's no way..."

Her voice sank, but I was thinking back to the time as a kid I'd done something nefarious to Lance Warcastle during one of our many feuds. Instead of taking the fight directly to him, I'd taken it to his house. Literally. I'd waited until dark and climbed an antenna tower to the roof with a roll of Grandma's Saran Wrap. I didn't want to kill them, just make life suck really, really bad. I'd wrapped their stink pipe and left their chimney alone. Lance had come to school for two days without washing. Apparently, his drains had stopped working well, and well... It took a plumber running a mechanical snake down it and failing to unblock things to figure it out. Then he'd gone to snake it from the roof and pulled the Saran Wrap off. The drains had worked after that.

I was thinking along those same lines myself, but instead of using the stink pipe, I WAS thinking of using the chimney, and not for what anybody would expect. Not anybody sane, that is. The trick was getting up there without being seen.

"I got to get on top of that roof," I whispered to Jessica, pulling the pack off and fishing around until I found two heavy, oblong objects.

"Do you want to see if it's safe getting everyone out?" Jessica asked quietly.

"How am I going to get Raider up the ladder?" I asked her.

She grunted, and I kept looking. I could tell there was a patrol around the small clearing where a few cabins had been erected. Henry had the nicest cabin of everyone there. It was hard to make out all the details in the dark, but it looked like on the far side of the clearing a number of holes were being dug by a few men, with two watching over things. With a start, I realized it was to bury the dead. We'd taken our toll on Henry's men and the newcomers, but nowhere near what Henry probably had with the residents of the MAG group.

Jessica opened her mouth to answer, but the relative quiet of the night was ripped apart as an explosion rocked the back of the cabin. Those near the front of the cabin either hit the ground on their own or were thrown from the concussion of the blast. Wood splinters flew in every direction, and I expected to see smoke, but after putting my face in the dirt for a good twenty seconds, I didn't see anything. The small valley erupted in shouts, and then as the man ran toward the back of the log cabin, gunfire rang out.

In the dark it was easy to tell from the muzzle flashes, but it seemed to be only one side was firing. Were they shooting into the dark hoping to run someone off? Was it that they thought we were attacking them? A million thoughts and plans ran through my mind, and I pulled my rifle up to use the scope to see if I could get an opportunity to take out Henry in the confusion.

"They're attacking Henry's," a voice came out of the radio.

We had it on softly and had been silent for much of the time since I'd taunted the leader. They probably didn't want to share sensitive information, figuring if Jessica and Linda Carpenter were with us, we would know their communications and have their encryption keys.

Jessica tapped me on the shoulder, and I rolled to

my side to look at her. "We gotta get out of here," Jessica whispered. "Let's go back to the armory."

"Why, do you know what's going on?"

"If I'm not mistaken, that was probably my mom down there."

WE BELLY CRAWLED ALONG THE EDGE OF THE TRAIL. Other than two shapes in the shadows, thrown by a flashlight on the main trail, we didn't see anyone. I thought about shooting one of the shapes with the silenced rifle, but Jessica shook her head. She told me this might be our best chance of getting down to the family and getting them out while everyone was distracted. We had no idea if the group that had left to go chase after the missing truck would be back to assist in the hunt for us. We'd just thrown a monkey wrench into everything. Once again.

The chatter we heard on the radio was sporadic, and it was highly confused. The only voice I didn't hear on the radio was Henry's. Another voice came on claiming they had heard a dog barking, but it was further down in the valley, a quarter-mile behind Henry's log cabin. That worked for us because that was the opposite direction of where we were heading. A new rough plan had formed, and it seemed to me that Jessica was probably right. It was good to get now, as the going was good to get, but my problem was I didn't know if we would be safe to go back to my grandparents' house.

I wanted to ask all of these questions, to get Jessica's feedback on everything, but time seemed to feel like it was running out. I could feel my heart beat, and my vision seemed to pulse in time with it. Ahead of us, we both abruptly paused our approaches as we heard something crashing through the brush ahead of us. The sound seemed to split in two, and we readied our guns as something, or someone came at us from two different directions. I had my gun leveled on a spot ten feet ahead of me, where I expected the man or woman to come running out of the brush. I heard Jess flick her safety off. I was doing the same as I heard a chuffing sound as something skid to a halt just out of my vision. A quiet but sharp bark reached my ears, and then Raider stepped out in front of me.

He let out one more quick bark and ran to me, and almost pulled me over in his excitement. I was able to flick the safety back on the rifle, and then rolled onto my back as much as the backpack would let me, making shushing noises. Jess let out a low whistle, and Yaeger broke brush just off to her right. I heard her let out a small laugh, and soon she was rolling on the ground with her dog as well.

"*Nein,*" I said, remembering the command, and Raider sat just two steps back, his tongue hanging out in a doggy grin.

He let out another chuff, and I turned to see that

Yaeger had done the same thing as Raider. Jess and I got to our knees slowly, and then she turned to me.

"How did he get out?"

"I don't know, but if he's out that must mean…"

"Raider," Grandpa said in a low voice, his words almost out of earshot.

"Buddy, you head back there, and we will all follow."

Jessica turned to Yaeger. "Roving sweep," she said in English.

It wasn't a command I'd ever heard her use before, but Yaeger took off in the bushes. Jessica and I both got to our feet and started following Raider, who would stop and wait for us. Yaeger was walking silently all around us, his nose to the ground. I could see his tail waving like a flag as he went about his job happily. I swatted at a mosquito, looking ahead in the gloom.

"Raider," Grandpa's voice came out of the dark about ten feet in front of us.

"Go," I whispered to him.

Raider let out a happy bark as he leapt forward. Jessica and I held our guns at the low ready position and came out onto the trail. I was gob smacked. Marshall and Linda were there, along with the entire group I'd left underground.

"Looks like you two finally got to go fishing," Marshall said by way of hello.

I looked at Jessica, then back at him. It was hard not to grin. There were so many things I wanted to say, so many words I wanted to speak, but Grandpa and Grandma shared sly looks.

"Fishing?" Linda asked.

"I'll tell you later," Jessica said without a hint of amusement.

The laughter that had started inside of me cut off. She shot me a cold look, then nodded for the trail. Marshall was carrying Mary gently like a doll. His gangly form didn't look sturdy enough to do it, but he wasn't even struggling. Raider sat at my feet and looked at the group with me. They looked drawn, tired. Something bad had gone here, and it had touched every one of us. If I saw my reflection, would I see the man I was becoming? The guy who coldly stomped the throat of the man who'd betrayed him? I shivered suddenly, not wanting to think about that.

"Wes," Linda said, "I need you to help carry Diesel."

"He's alive?" Jessica asked, pushing forward, letting out a low whistle.

The brush about ten feet down the trail rustled, and a low whine came. It sounded the way a rusty bolt would sound when it was finally turning without penetrating oil. Jessica beat me there by a long shot, but I found the big dog laying on his side. Three puckered holes were visible on his right flank, two were right over the shoulder blade, but the third was higher up, with what looked like an exit wound that didn't quite just skimmed just inside the skin. He wagged his nubbin of a tail, licking Jessica's hand. She handed me her rifle and tried to lift him, but I knew she couldn't. Raider was sniffing at the wounds, making a low sound in his chest that wasn't quite a growl.

I got it. She'd remembered what I'd done, and she didn't really want my help, even though this should have been my job. I was too ashamed to say anything until I took off my pack and nudged her with my boot. I handed her the two rifles as she silently tried to wipe tears away.

"I'm only here to help the big guy," I said quietly.

Diesel made a groaning sound, and when I got down on my knees and slid my arms under his body, Raider chose that moment to let out a small bark and lick me on the side of the face and ear. I rubbed my ear on my shoulder and braced for what I knew was going to hurt the both of us, Diesel and me. I stood slowly as Diesel started whining. He didn't snap at me, or his wounds, but I knew the big lug couldn't help but cry from the pain. We'd have to get some compression on the wounds, dig out any lead, get him stitched closed...

"You got him?" Jessica asked.

"Yeah, I won't let anything happen to him."

"Thank you," she said softly.

The night behind us was mostly silent, with the occasional crackle of voices from a distant radio.

9

THE MOTOR POOL had been empty of guards and people. Several of the trucks, including the old troop transport, were gone, probably out looking for us. Instead, we were able to climb into Linda's old Ford with a long bed. Linda, Marshall, and Mary rode up front, the little girl asleep and boneless from exhaustion and probably needing to heal. The rest of us rode in the bed of the pickup. Emily, Jessica, my grandparents and I. Grandma had the best seat of all, sitting on two of the backpacks that the group had appropriated from the armory. Emily was off to the side, wearing her own backpack and carrying what looked like a lever action rifle.

There was something savage in her tonight. I had expected her to be the one to carry Mary out, but the small woman had let Marshall take the lead.

"How'd you find Marshall?" I asked Grandpa,

breaking the silence as we crept along the dirt road in the dark.

"He found Linda and helped her set off the diversion. They figured on hitting the armory to get Jessica free, and then were gonna get out of Dodge."

"How did you guys...?"

"Followed your dog. He wouldn't stop and went looking for you after a while. Did you know your damn dog can climb ladders?"

I grinned in the dark. "I suspected."

"Anyway, I found Linda and Marshall and their dogs, and Marshall came down and helped carry the little girl out."

"I would have done it, but the rungs were too far apart," Emily said, something bitter in her voice.

"Would have banged the girl's head up, and she can't have that none while she's a healing," Grandma said softly, trying to play peacemaker.

"Short girl problems," Emily said curtly.

The middle back window slid open. "Linda wants to know how the ride is?"

"Good so far," Grandma said, "bumps aren't bad."

We'd been running without lights. Apparently, a while back, Linda and Dave had rewired all of the lights, running lights, brake lights and backup lights, to switches. You turn them on, everything worked as normal. You turn the switches off, nothing lights up. I appreciated the foresight, but I didn't understand how Linda was driving in the pitch black. There were a lot of gaps, and I wanted to be filled in, but I wasn't sure this was a good time.

"Is your buddy Lester going to shoot first and ask questions later?" Linda's voice asked from the cab of the truck.

"He might," Grandpa said. "That's why I told you not to turn down his property."

With a pang, I suddenly realized that my truck was still at the compound. Dammit. We could have split up, and Linda could have followed me. Now... I heard a motor rev in the distance and turned to see the glow of lights somewhere behind us.

"Uhhh, guys, we might have a problem." My words were almost lost with the creaking of the suspension and the crunch of gravel while we traveled maybe twenty-five miles an hour.

"What?" Jessica asked, then she saw it too as a set of headlights crested the hill behind us. "Uh oh," she mumbled, bringing her carbine up. "Mom, we've got company coming."

Linda cursed, and there was a flurry of movement inside the cab.

"Take the wheel a moment," I heard her say, and the truck lurched then steadied.

"Got it," she said to Marshall.

"Mommy, I don't feel so good," Mary murmured through the window.

"I know, honey, just try to go back to sleep," Emily called back.

Raider and Yaeger both were laying near the back

of the pickup's tailgate with Diesel laying on a tarp in the middle of all of us. Emily wedged the carbine down and got her backpack out. It was dark colored, olive drab, if I had to guess. It clanked as she dug through things and pulled out a massive revolver and set it on the bag before picking up the lever gun again.

I passed the silenced rifle to Grandpa, who nodded.

"Is it them?" Grandma asked.

I nodded, almost positive. The radio crackled, and I plugged in the earpiece so I could hear.

"Passed my position three minutes ago, heading west ... over."

"They've got lookouts calling in where we are."

Jess cursed. "Who's got NVG gear?"

"I'm wearing the set from Wes' backpack," Linda's mom said from the cab, the truck accelerating.

"Damn," Jess swore again.

"You don't need no fancy specs," Grandpa told them. "They're coming in trucks with the lights on, right?"

"Yeah?" Jessica asked.

"Unless people shoot at us as we drive by, it's the trucks we've got to worry about, right?"

Jess nodded. Headlights crested the hill, washing the bed of the truck in a bright light, and I could hear their motor roar, the driver hitting the gas.

"Found them, in Linda Carpenter's truck, west, heading west. Over."

"How far back are you?" Henry's voice came over the radio.

"Closing fast." The truck's motor revved audibly.

I looked at the M4 I'd taken off of the dead man in the Crater of Diamonds and flicked the selector switch off safe. The dump pouch was heavy, and if I could have figured out how to wear the grenades like they did in the movies, I'd be decked out in those. Instead, I reached in the bag and pulled out two with my left hand, handing Jess one of them.

"It's them?" she asked, nodding at my earpiece.

"It's them," I confirmed.

Grandpa and Grandma slid as far as they could against the back cab of the truck, pulling Diesel with them and calling for Yaeger and Raider. I winced as Linda bottomed the truck out on a pothole. In the dark I couldn't see them coming and I nearly lost hold of the grenade. That would be bad news.

"Ok, when I tell you, pull the pin," Jess said, showing me, "and throw it about ten yards from the truck. Should give us enough time. Ready?"

I nodded as a third set of headlights joined in the chase. I could hear things on the radio, but my body had seemingly slowed down, and I wasn't hearing things very well. Out of the side of my vision, I could see Emily raise up on a knee with the rifle and started firing two aimed rounds. Jess pulled the pin, and I followed suit. We let the spoons fly, and I chucked mine about the same moment she did. I reached down for my carbine and brought it up to my shoulder. I was about to start firing at the growing glow of high beams when two explosions rocked the night.

The rear end of the lead truck shot sideways with the explosion and turned it into a machine of death. I had enough time to recognize Lance's truck before it started rolling our direction, almost as if it wanted to catch up. I noticed the bed had a few men in it, who were either thrown when the truck first started rolling or were smashed and pulped into the road. Behind it, two more trucks could be made out in the moonlight and headlights of the rear truck. Lance's truck was starting to slow when the middle truck revved the engine, surging forward. His truck was smashed aside as the duce and a half troop carrier came after us.

I started firing. I didn't know anything other than military vehicles except they were big, ugly, and probably armored. I put a few rounds over the left side headlight toward the middle of the windshield with seemingly no effect. Linda swerved, and I nearly lost my footing when Emily fell into me. One of the dogs was barking its head off and a muzzle flash on the side of the road caught my eye. I brought my carbine around but broke off as Jess fired on it. Emily grabbed my left arm and pulled herself to her feet; she'd been thrown by the maneuver herself. She didn't have the weight advantage that I had to keep me mostly planted.

I grabbed under her armpit, steadying her, and then got to my feet and started firing at the truck that was gaining on us. They had a top speed of what? Sloth?

"We need more speed!" I shouted and started firing at what I hoped was the radiator.

"Do you have any more grenades?" Jess shouted from next to me.

"Yeah," I said, watching as my shots made the driver of the big truck swerve to try to avoid the incoming fire.

Emily's rifle went off, and bright sparks flew up from the hood, and I saw the glass spider web. Had I even hit the windshield before? She worked the lever as I started firing at the glass again. The truck swerved more.

"We replaced the glass with lightweight bulletproof glass," Jess said, coming up with the grenade.

She pulled the pin and dropped it over the side, with the truck almost twenty feet behind us. I didn't know how fast we were going, but I realized that while I was sweating profusely, I was strangely cool.

"Hold on," Linda yelled, and we all braced ourselves as the truck took a sharp right turn onto a paved road.

Then she hit the gas, almost pitching us forward until we compensated for the movement.

"You sit still, you big asshole," Grandma was chiding Raider.

Grandpa was holding the silenced rifle in the air, but at some point, Diesel had crawled into his lap, effectively pinning him in place. The big truck made the turn just as the grenade went off, lighting up the side of the truck. I was surprised I didn't hear screams from the back. I didn't know if there were men in the back the way there had been men in the bed of Lance's truck. What did happen, though, was the driver caught in mid-turn, over compensated, and the rear end swung the entire truck in a 360 degree turn. The rear tires on one side had been shredded by the grenade. We had a moment to breathe, but there was still another truck coming.

"That will make them more cautious," Jess said, changing magazines in her carbine.

She'd emptied it at some point, and I hadn't even heard. I dropped my magazine and saw a few rounds left in it. I switched it out for a fresh one and looked back. Grandma and Grandpa were ok, but the dogs were unhappy about being held back, except for Diesel who looked like he was trying to smother Grandpa with his body. Emily was searching through her backpack, her rifle in her left hand.

"What do you need?" I asked her.

"More cartridges," she said, her voice panicked.

I knelt and held the bag open for her with my left hand. She reached in and pulled a box of shells out just as I heard Jessica start firing, and the rounds were coming out like a buzz saw. Emily and I both jerked at the sudden gunfire, and she dropped the box. Cursing, she dropped the rifle in the bed and rose up, the large stainless-steel revolver in her hand. I had half a moment to think WTF? This handgun made Dirty Harry's look like a toy pistol. The other thing I observed was that she was holding the gun as if it weighed nothing. Even looking at this thing made me wonder how such a tiny human could—

She fired just as I was raising up to do the same. Flame left the barrel for a good six feet, almost blinding me. Jessica stopped firing when I just put a few rounds into the truck that seemed to be slowing down and backing off. Emily's hand cannon went off again, and it hit something solidly metal, making steam erupt from the front of the truck that was definitely coming to a stop. Grinding sounds and a loud bang precluded it stopping half in and out of the grass median.

Jessica tapped the roof of the truck and called for her mom to stop.

"We don't know if there's any more," Linda said.

"Just stop a sec, would you?"

I was putting my hand over the earpiece, listening, but all I was getting was constant static. Whoever had the radio wasn't transmitting right now. I shrugged when Jessica looked at me, but Linda was already slowing.

Jessica didn't wait for the truck to come to a complete stop, she hopped out gracefully and whistled. Yaeger leapt over the side of the truck, and they headed for the darkness of the median. Stay? Go with? She was the expert on this stuff. Then again, I wasn't a slouch myself. Years of hunting, stalking prey, and being wary because Johnny Law would be on my ass otherwise had given me a similar if different skillset.

"Come on, Raider," I said, and stepped over the tailgate.

No jumping acrobatics for me or my dog, so I lowered the tailgate and let my buddy off.

"No heroics," Linda said through the rolled down window.

"What are you going back there for? We can just get going down the road," Grandpa said, half statement, half question.

"I think she's... I don't know what she's doing. I just have to go."

"Be careful, grandson," Grandma said with surprising gentleness.

"I will. Raider, let's go, other side."

"Mary, how you doing?" Emily asked.

"I'm ok, that was scary, but I could see the fireworks in the mirror!"

"Good. Marshall, Linda, I'll be right back," Emily said.

I heard the bed of the truck creak and saw Emily had jumped off, and she was following close behind me. We got on the left side of the road in the grass median and started walking. The headlights of the truck winked off, and I knelt, closing my eyes, willing my night vision to come back. Emily must have as well, because I felt her hand on my left shoulder, her breath tickling the back of my neck.

"You don't do anything stupid," Emily whispered, her words tickling my ears.

I opened my eyes and wasn't as blinded by the after

glare of the headlights. "I won't. Stay close, Raider'll have point, and if he starts the dance, give him room. Do not shoot my dog." It was a word salad of ideas. My body felt like I'd had a shot of pure caffeine after the greatest session in a bounce house with an entire college cheerleading squad. I felt dry mouthed, excited, nervous, strong, shaky, jittery, and I was having a hard time focusing with her breath on my neck. I stood fast, a little too fast, bumping into her. Raider ran over, licking her in the face until she pushed him back, holding that monstrous revolver.

"How can you shoot that thing?" I asked her.

"Cock the hammer, aim, pull the trigger?"

I could make out the shape of the truck in the darkness and heard Jess calling out commands to Yaeger as they got close. I started walking as she pulled the side door open. A body rolled out, then there was a scrambling motion from the passenger seat as somebody who'd been playing dead made a break for it.

"Támadás," I barked as the man stumbled to his feet and started running.

Raider took off like a shot, and I forgot all pretense of cover and started running. I heard Jess bark a similar command and both dogs snarled. Yaeger got to the man first, pulling him down after a running leap and latch on his arm. Raider was there a couple seconds later, pulling on the man's free hand, both dogs shaking their heads the way a terrier would shake a rat.

Jessica got there first and gave them the break off

command. I got there a couple seconds later as the man pulled his arms to his sides, rolling into a ball. Jessica snapped on a flashlight, lighting up the man's face. He was covered in blood and gore, though the only wound I saw was what looked like a crease that cut a line on the bottom of his chin.

"Stop, stop, I surrender," he said, over and over, his words half sob, half in fear.

I'd seen the truck had been empty when I'd run past, the bed as well, so my focus was now on the man on the ground.

"Who are you?" Jessica asked him. She let her carbine hang down by the sling, and had one hand holding the flashlight, the other having drawn one of the 1911s we'd liberated.

"Aaron," the man said, gasping, still curled up in a fetal position.

He was older than me, his sandy blond hair streaked with gray at the temples. He had on black BDUs like the newcomers we'd seen, his gear looking like swat gear. He had a knife and holstered pistol, but he didn't look like he remembered he even had them on, and if he went for them, he'd be ventilated by the three of us.

"Get up," Jessica said.

The radio in my ear crackled funny, and I pressed my hand to my ear. All I got was more garbage, so I pulled the PTT cord out of the radio. Immediately the garbage became words. Somewhere along the way, I'd damaged the cord end, or maybe the radio, but the words coming out of the speaker were clear.

"Status report, over." The voice didn't sound like Henry's, it sounded like the boss at the Crater of Diamonds. Spider?

"Lost contact with the three trucks giving chase. They passed our last lookout on that road. Coordinating with others to see if the bastards pop up, over." This transmission was further away by the sound of things.

Aaron looked at us, and he slowly relaxed as he sat up, putting his hands on his head. Raider puffed his fur out as he growled. I could see the man shiver as he looked at what fanged death might have been or might yet be. Yaeger was sitting next to Jessica, looking calmer than my pup. He was coiled and ready, but I could still tell he was waiting for the next command.

"You have location of Aaron's truck?" Spider asked.

"No, they passed us two minutes ago. Heavy gunfire and explosions could be heard from my position. Not sure if they ambushed them or were ambushed, over."

"We'll send out search parties at first light. Stay in place until you're relieved. Switch frequencies as planned. Over and Out."

"Out."

"Looks like your buddies think you're dead," I told him.

"I might as well be," he said.

"Who are you, and where are you from?" Emily asked, reminding me she was still right there.

"Aaron, came from Texarkana." His reply was short, and I could see his confidence coming back slowly, making me wary.

"Raider, if he so much as moves, tear his throat out," I said, hoping the threat sounded as mean to the man as it did me.

My dog knew no such command, but he'd had two people set their trained Shepherds loose on him, so he may or may not know it was a ruse, but I was pretty sure Yaeger knew a command for that.

"Who are you with? Your group?" Jessica asked.

"You don't know? You're so screwed," he said, smiling.

"Military? Law enforcement?" I asked.

He turned to look at me, squinting against Jessica's flashlight, which was probably blinding him. "We're all former military, half special forces. We all joined up to be trained and then went to work for the same PMC."

"PMC?" I asked him.

"Private Military Contractor," Jess told me. "What's your mission, and how many are working with you?"

"My mission? Shit, right now it's to get food, a base, and stay alive. As far as how many of us are there? Depends on who you ask. We joined up with the locals about a week ago and have been filtering in more and more every day."

"How many are with you?" Jessica repeated.

"More than a couple, less than a few?" he said, grinning.

The crease on his chin was dripping blood onto his black BDU shirt, where it soaked in.

"You want to die on the side of the road?" I asked him. "Trust me, we're not cops."

"No, from my intel, you're Jessica," he said pointing to her, "and you'd be Wes, the chemist, and I'm guessing that wildcat with the big gun is the nutjob who got away from Lance's boys."

"Nutjob?" Emily asked, cocking the big revolver and raising it up.

"Kept smacking your head into the wall, wasn't happy with the attention you were going to get. Almost bit the finger off a guy—"

His head exploded like a watermelon getting hit by a sledge hammer. Both dogs and human handlers were startled.

"I'm not a nutjob," Emily said, turning and walking to the truck and leaning inside. "You need anything from here?"

Jess' hand tapped me on the arm, and I gave her a nod. The little woman might not be a nutjob, but she was something scary.

"We need the radios," Jessica called, then started the grisly work of stripping the man of anything useful.

I helped, taking extra magazines, a pocketknife, a sheath knife, his pistol and combat belt. The rest of the stuff didn't really look like anything we'd need, and once we turned the body over, we found his radio clipped to the back of his pants. He'd never had a chance to use it.

"Got one, and a charger for it," Emily called out. She'd tucked another pistol into her waistband, had a carbine slung over her shoulders like Jess and I did, and was holding a small canvas sack that rattled.

"Taking the guns and ammo. Are we going to go back for the rest?" she asked, nodding in the direction we'd come from.

"No, we've stayed long enough. You should go check on Mary."

Emily gave us both a look, then let out a sigh and started jogging.

"Raider, go with her," I told my buddy who'd been standing just outside the circle of blood that was quickly drying.

Raider sneezed at me, but he got to his feet.

"I think he just told you bullshit," Jess said, spitting what looked like a glob of blood out of her mouth.

"You ok?" I asked her.

"Banged my face in the truck. Think a stitch tore, hurts. Yaeger, go with," she said pointing.

"Raider, go with her." I pointed again.

He grumbled at me and started trotting after Yaeger.

"You trying to get me alone?" Jessica asked.

"I was trying to make sure ... what she just did ... that sorta freaked me out."

"You stomping on Jimmy's throat sort of freaked me out," Jessica said.

I'd been moving closer to her, to try to hug her, maybe steal a kiss, but that stopped me. I looked in her eyes, and she held my gaze for a moment, then she turned and started walking away, leaving me in the darkness. Not wanting to make anybody wait, I headed out myself.

GRANDPA HAD SNUCK AHEAD. Good thing too, because Lester had heard the truck coming for a good half a mile before we had gotten there, and had been waiting. When he'd come back, he was quiet, drawn, and paler than normal under the glare of our flashlights.

"What's wrong?" Grandma asked him immediately.

"Follow me in," Grandpa said, clicking his flashlight on and motioning in the darkness with his light.

In the darkness another light clicked on and flashed back at us, making a circular motion. Grandpa made a 'come on' gesture, and Linda started the truck up and followed as he shambled slowly down the long, winding gravel driveway.

"What's going on here?" Marshall asked from inside the truck.

"Probably being careful," Emily said, her arms through the middle window separating the cab from the bed, her hands working her daughter's hair distractedly.

"Knowing old Lester, he's probably got this place trapped, or got some guys in the bushes watching us," I said to everybody who could hear me over the barely idling engine.

"That ain't the half of it, look," Jessica said, pointing.

Grandma cursed as she saw what we were going past. I didn't know how Jessica had picked it up out of the dark, but it looked like a chunk of old well casing sticking out of the ground, angled up slightly. I got a chill as I realized what that might be, and again was amazed Jessica had seen it, even with the lights rolling past it. It had been expertly hidden by the brush. I was going to ask her how she'd picked that out, but the light had already moved on. In the bed, Jessica moved away from me. I couldn't say I blamed her.

The light had shown that she had torn a couple stitches loose in today's ordeals, and a smear of blood had dried to a crust from mid cheek to the bottom of her chin.

"Go ahead and turn on the headlights," Grandpa called, turning his flashlight off.

He moved to the side of the driveway, and as we were riding past, he reached a hand up to me. I locked my hand over his wrist, and he did the same, putting his other one on the bed of the truck. I pulled as he jumped and pushed off. He must have had a foot on the back bumper, because he sailed into the bed easily.

I was so surprised that I almost fell over backward because I had braced myself to haul him in.

"I got it," Grandpa said, "unless you're planning on playing grab ass with me."

"Not even," I said, grinning, at the same time as Raider let out a happy bark.

That perked up Diesel, and the big dog lifted his head off Grandma's lap and looked around. The movement made him whine, which ended up making Yaeger belly crawl to his buddy and sniff at the quick makeshift bandages.

"Stop here," Grandpa said.

Emily walked to my side, slinging her rifle and stuffing the big stainless-steel revolver into her backpack before putting that across her shoulder. All that weight had me wondering how strong the little woman was. Jessica saw me watching and rolled her eyes. I was going to tell her it wasn't what she thought, but she'd hopped off the back of the bed without touching the side. She landed in a crouch, then raised up and lowered the tailgate.

Yaeger and Raider ran to the back as I crawled over the side less gracefully. I'd planned on using the tire as a step down, but my foot slipped, almost causing me to smack my head on the bed of the truck. Jessica gave her dogs the stay command as Diesel tried to move, but Grandma patted him and scooted out from under him. The cab of the truck emptied, and Marshall got out. Emily was right there and handed him her backpack, reaching in to scoop up Mary. The little girl had fallen asleep again. I clicked my flashlight on for a moment and saw that her throat had stayed sewn shut in all that craziness.

I didn't understand what had been happening. Only the first chase truck had held men in the bed, and I hadn't been for sure they were even shooting at us. The men on the side of the road had, but all things considered, I was at a bit at a loss as to why they hadn't opened up. Private Military Contractors? They had fully automatic toys, and their numbers alone could have probably ripped us to shreds. Had us tossing grenades, taking out the biggest threats. I didn't know, but what I did know was Jessica and Linda were talking heatedly with Grandpa, who was standing in the wash from the headlights.

Both ladies had tear-streaked faces, and Linda's face was beet red. I had no doubt the conversation was about me, then I realized what an arrogant thought that was to have. Not everything revolved around me. Grandma patted me on the shoulder, and when I turned, she held out a hand. I gave it to her, and she wobbly walked to the back of the truck and sat on the tailgate and scooted off.

"If this wasn't such a cock up, that chase ride might have been fun," she said with a wry grin.

"I... I honestly haven't even processed things yet," I admitted. "It was so fast, so quick. I still have the shakes."

I held my hands up to show her and saw my arms had broken out into gooseflesh. Something tender came into Grandma's eyes, and she ruffled my hair like she used to when I was a boy, then she looked away as we heard Grandpa say, "Well, that's your call," and he walked up to us, clearly disgusted.

"Raider, here," I called.

The truck lurched as my pup jumped out and ran to me, bumping my hip with his head, and rubbing his ear and snout on my side.

"Marking you as his," Emily said, walking up, a sleeping Mary in her arms.

"I think so," I told her. "Or he really missed me."

"Load up," Linda said abruptly from the front of the truck.

"Where are you going to park it?" I asked, noticing Jessica looking at me, her face drawn tight.

"Hello," Lester said, coming out of the gloom.

"There you are. I was wondering where'd you gotten off to," Grandpa said.

"Making sure everybody knows you were coming in and a million other things," Les said with a quick snort. "Wes, how you doing?"

"Good," I told him, wondering who 'everybody' was.

"Ma'am... Uh... Miss Jessica, are you ok? Do you need to see—"

"I'm fine," she said. "Mom and I need to bugout. We safe to leave?"

"You're not staying with—"

"No," Linda and Jessica chorused.

My hands were somewhat free. I'd slung the M4

and had my pack back on, so Emily nudged me and offered up Mary. I took the little girl gently and held her close to me. She smelled like disinfectant, lye soap, and a hint of something fruity. She'd obviously been bathed or had showered while we were all kept underground, but she wasn't the grimy little ragamuffin I'd first met, just a precious and fragile one.

She let out a sigh and wrapped an arm around my neck, murmuring something about Tubbies and SpongeBob in her sleep. Grandma put a comforting hand on my shoulder and gave the newly formed knot of muscles a squeeze. Grandpa and Les opened and closed their mouths like they were going to speak, and then didn't.

"Don't call us, we'll call you," Linda Carpenter said. "We're leaving," she told Lester.

The old cutout man nodded, looking at me, confused. I had no words, I was at a loss. Jessica walked back and closed the tailgate, then climbed up and over before Yaeger tried to push past her and sit with Raider. Thinking his name was enough for my buddy to let out a low rumble that ended with a 'ru ru ru' sound. I tried to brush my free hand against his head, but Mary shifted. Emily walked up to Jessica's side of the bed of the truck. I tensed, because I could see the wild side about to rip loose from the small woman.

"After all he's done for us, for you, for everyone, you're just going walk away?"

"He murdered my father," Jessica said.

"He's lucky I don't put a bullet in his skull," Linda

growled, her face red in the glow of backwash from the headlights, her face more tear-streaked than before.

"You might want to look around you, young missy," Les said quietly.

Forms came out of the darkness. They were dressed in woodland camo, some of them with the old BDU pattern that had gone out of style during the Korean War. Linda's red face went pale as about thirty forms converged on the truck, their rifles at the low and ready. None of them spoke a word, but Jess hissed in surprise.

"I think you'll find that'd be an unwise idea," Les said laconically, "especially when surrounded by friends of the Flaggs."

One man stepped forward, and with a start, I recognized him. Then a second stepped forward, carrying what looked like a Remington 700 police edition. Deputy Rolston and Sheriff Jackson.

"Ain't gonna be bloodshed tonight," the sheriff said, a statement more than a question.

"We're out of here," Jessica said, smacking the top of the truck.

"Wait," I said, walking to the driver's side door where Linda sat. "I want my NVGs," I told her.

Linda muttered under her breath but handed them over to me from the front seat. I took them in one hand while she dug around, then threw the charger my way. It hit the ground, and I winced. Grandma picked it up as the door was slammed.

"Linda—"

"My husband is dead, haven't you done enough?" she asked me.

"As much of a badass as you and your family are, don't you think a lot of this could have been prevented? Your husband was going to shoot my dog."

"He's a *dog*, and my husband is *dead*!" The last came out in a shout.

"I'm sorry for that," I told her. "I wish I could take it all back, but you shouldn't be blaming me. You should be blaming Henry."

I heard a couple of metallic clicks behind me as the men who'd ghosted out of the darkness flicked off their safeties.

"He might have caused it, but you pulled the trigger." Any other words were cut off as she turned on the truck and put it in reverse.

Several people stepped out of the way as the truck reversed until there was a clear spot in the brush that lined Les' driveway and then turned around. I watched her headlights until they were distant in my field of vision. Raider howled, a low mournful sound, but loud enough to make me break out into goose bumps again. Yaeger or Diesel howled back, punctuated with several barks.

Just like that, they were gone, and I was pretty sure that I'd just been dumped.

11

THE NIGHT WENT by in a hurry, and Les had us all bunk down in his living room. I hadn't minded as it looked like he had a houseful, or several. I had picked a spot on the floor, near my grandparents, after I'd given Mary to her mother. We'd fallen asleep after somebody with EMT training had checked out both Mary and me. I was almost too tired from the adrenaline let down to care or even notice. I also noticed that my blanket had been pulled up, and Emily lay next to me, her back pressed against mine as she whispered to Mary.

How the little girl had survived all of this was a mystery to me, but I was thankful she had. My eyes were heavy and scratchy. It felt like I'd been using sandpaper on my pupils, but I didn't say anything as everyone was falling asleep. I'd heard the expression too tired to do anything, and I now knew what that felt like. I desperately wanted sleep, but it was elusive.

"Westley," Les' voice came out of the fog that my brain was floating in.

"Yeah?" I said, my voice thick.

"We got to talk," Les said softly.

I tried to sit up but realized somebody was laying across my lap. I tried to get up slowly, so as not to disturb Emily or Mary, but found it was Raider instead.

"Get up, you lug," I said, moving my legs in an effort to wake my dog up.

He let out a loud snore, but I saw him crack an eye and look my way.

"Get up," I said, looking around, seeing a good fifteen or twenty people under blankets and in sleeping bags all around us.

Raider made a rumbling noise, rolled off me, farted, and then started snoring again, in that order. I waved the fumes away from my face and followed Lester who was tiptoeing his way to the kitchen. I bumped into somebody, and Deputy Rolston pulled the covers off his face. He'd been a Coleman cocoon a moment before.

"Sorry," I said, "Not quite got my feet under me yet."

"It's ok," he said, pulling the covers over his head.

"Come on," Les said quietly.

I followed him into his kitchen. I'd been in here once, about twenty years ago when Grandpa and he were the biggest outlaws this side of Arkansas. The faded linoleum floors had been changed out at some point, but the chipped Formica countertops and cupboards were all the same. I remembered as a kid sitting at his snack bar on spindly metal stools, sipping on a coke while Grandpa and he talked about business. He motioned to the same stool I'd sat on as a kid, and with a touch of nostalgia, I sat, feeling like I was almost a teen again.

"Fill me in," Les told me, sitting across from me.

I rubbed my eyes again. They felt like they had crusties spread all over and had scratched lines in my retinas. I was about to talk when he got up suddenly and went to his stove and grabbed a percolator and an old porcelain mug with the Jolly Green Giant printed on it in faded green. I watched, almost drooling as he poured a mug that looked to be half road tar and all savory, bitter goodness. An oxymoron, I know, but my entire attention focused on that mug and didn't let up until I'd taken my first sip.

I could feel my blood vessels expanding, soaking in the first vestiges of caffeine that I'd had in a while. It was amazing and wonderful and scary how fast an old addiction had reared its ugly head and screamed in a rather insistent voice ... MOAR!

"So Jessica and Linda's place... The guy who was running it was hooked up with Private Military Contractors, who are the guys who sort of took over from Lance's crew at the crater. Most of their group was killed after I tried to break out of there the first time. They know where we live, so we came here first, hoping to lay low for a day or so. We're pretty sure we weren't followed."

"You tried to get away from them more than once?" Les asked.

I downed the scalding hot coffee, putting the mug down on the Formica with a loud tap.

"Yeah, the first time was pretty ugly. The second time was tonight, and we broke out everyone else who was willing to go."

"What do you mean was willing to go?" he asked me softly.

"They killed the rest. The rest of Henry's group had no idea, except a handful. They slaughtered them."

"How bad was it? Where is Dave Carpenter?"

Knew him, did he?

"He's dead," I said, and I couldn't look him in the eye as I said it.

"I'm guessing he was part of the crew that ... wait, but Linda and Jessica—"

"They weren't part of it. Henry was blackmailing Dave, and when he tried shooting Raider..."

I heard a chuff from the doorway, and my dog came in, stretching his legs one at a time before he trotted to my side and looked up at my coffee cup longingly.

"Can I get my boy some water?" I asked, sliding off my stool.

"Just sit down. I saw you getting checked out, you took some damage some time back," he said pointing at my shoulder.

"Jessica jumped in front of her dad..." I blurted out, but I couldn't finish the words.

"I saw she'd been shot. You?" he asked.

"Yeah, went through both cheeks. The slug expanded going out and took him in the face."

My body was burning, my face was red. Les grunted and took a bowl out and started filling it with water.

"I'm sorry, Wes," he said softly.

"Yeah."

WE DRANK COFFEE, AND I FILLED HIM IN ON everything that had happened since I'd last seen him. The sheriff's department had disbanded itself and gone AWOL, joining up with Lester. Some of the guys out there were former military, active military, and various friends and family that hadn't been happy with how the government had been running things. They had needed a place to congregate and set up until they could get good intel. As Les kept asking me questions, I realized he was pumping me for information as much as he was drawing me out of my funk.

Lester had always been my grandpa's contact and friend, but I'd always felt a fondness for the old guy, like an uncle I'd never had. My grandparents, as much as Les, knew all my secrets and had helped me as much as he could when it came to contacts and odd jobs. It was actually Les who'd got me the contact as a kid to buy the diamonds from the Crater.

"You know, now, that money is basically worthless, so someday, something is going to have to become the new basis for trade as people struggle to get things going again," I babbled.

"You were just thinking about old times, weren't you? That thirty-carat diamond?"

I grinned and nodded.

"Right now, I think the best thing for trade is the basics. Food, medication, booze, cigarettes. I'd say ammunition, but you don't want to trade it, and have it used against you."

"I was thinking the same thing," I told him. "But I was remembering back when you hooked me up with old man Jenkins."

"I can't believe you found that big honker just sitting there. Crazy thing. You hear of tourists finding them randomly, but never the locals."

"The locals probably already know who to sell to and keep it quiet," I told him ruefully.

"That's true, probably a few people over the years have hit big. Is that how you paid for college?"

"No, it's what we used to fix the well and get new tin on the roof." I grinned, feeling a tad proud and glad for a change in subject.

"New tin roof won't do no good, if people come in there and burn you out."

"All my preps and storage..." I moaned.

"That's part of what I wanted to talk to you about,"

Les said quietly. "I'm going to talk to your grandpa as well, already mentioned it to him, but we've got a good forty people here, mostly men, but a couple family groups."

I looked at him, shocked.

"I know, half are on watch right now, setting up defenses and spying on the movements of people coming into the area. Problem we have here is that I don't have as much land as y'all, and this side of the hills is all stony. I haven't run a tiller anywhere except my kitchen garden in years. Soil's no good either. I was wondering…"

"You want to relocate to the homestead?" I asked, surprised.

"Not forever, but at some point, we have to produce our own food or starve. Some folks here are like you and your grandparents, they put up for hard times. They stashed food when the government stooges came through, and we'll have to get that, but it's just not sustainable here, and I'm worried this won't be over any time soon."

"'This', being the no power, anarchy, and chaos?"

"There's been enough chaos and killing, but I fear things are about to get worse."

I thought about that, and the guy Emily had killed, and nodded in agreement.

"We put in a big garden this year, and if somebody has been keeping up on picking eggs, we should be ok for a while, but I don't have enough for forty—"

"I know," he said, putting his hands up placatingly,

"but with all these people coming into the area, we need a place we can lay in some crops and defend. You getting burned out of your homestead would hurt all the decent survivors left in the area. You know what I mean?"

I did, and I didn't. As far as defensible places go, ours sort of sucked. We were on the bottom of a hill, and it would take digging defensive positions into the high ground and a massive amount of manpower and firepower to protect it. Then I realized suddenly we did have the room, and everything else we needed, if we pooled resources. I grinned as Les topped up my coffee cup.

"To your health," Les grinned, pulling a flask out that looked suspiciously familiar and poured some into my coffee before doctoring his up as well, "and to better times."

"To better times," I said, clinking cups.

The old familiar warmth of the shine was almost as welcome as the caffeine. This time I didn't sip it and took a good sized gulp.

"Mister Westley?" a small voice asked.

I looked and Mary was standing in the kitchen doorway. I put my cup down and held out my hands. She came to us and shyly held her arms up to me. She was six, but apparently not too old to want to be held and comforted. I pushed my cup back with my forearm and picked her up and held her to me.

"How's your neck, Hun?" I asked her softly.

"Hurts, talking worse," she said softly.

"I know what you need," Les said getting up. "Ovaltine!"

"Yuck," she told him, and judging by the look on Lester's face, she'd made a face of her own.

He walked to his sink, got a cup from the cupboard, and filled it. I was shocked. His tap worked.

"How do you have water?" I asked him.

"Cistern up the hill. Spring fed. Why?"

"Safe water is going to become a precious resource soon," I told him.

"That gives me an idea," Lester said with a grin.

"What's that?" I asked as he handed the cup of water to Mary.

She took it in both hands and drank deeply. We both waited. I don't know where the urge came from, but I ran my fingers through her hair, smoothing down the bed head. She leaned back into my chest.

"My daddy never would do that," she said softly. "Thank you for helping me and my mommy."

"You're welcome, sweetheart. I'm just truly sorry you got hurt."

"Why are you sorry?" she asked, turning on my leg so she could see me.

"You got hurt. If I had stayed, none of this would have happened." I was looking at her throat, the area that had been stitched shut looked angry and red around the edges.

"Mister Westley, you saved us. Momma said so, and so do I. It hurts, but Momma said you gave me your blood, so you and I are related now, just like Momma gave me blood and we're related too. But I came out of my Momma's tummy."

Lester looked at me hard, and then he must have gotten something in his eye because he wiped them and got off his stool and went to the sink.

"You didn't tell me that," he said softly.

"I'm was a blood donor," I explained. "She almost..."

"I can see that," Les said.

"Momma said Mister Westley almost gave me all his blood. I hope he doesn't have something yucky. Momma always said boys have cooties. Mister Westley is a man, though. I don't know how long cooties infect boys. I hope I don't get cooties. Do you think I'll get cooties from you, Mister Westley?"

Something between a laugh and a sob escaped my lips as I tried to respond. Instead, I grabbed my coffee cup and downed it.

"Refill?" Les asked, holding up the flask.

I nodded.

Les took my cup to the propane stove and refilled the cup from the percolator, then brought it back. It was half full. The other half he refilled from Grandpa's flask. I reached down and hugged Mary tight. I had something in my eyes this time and wiped them when I released the hug.

"I haven't had cooties since 2004," I told her.

"That was forever ago. You must be ancient, older than my momma!"

115

"Age is just a number," Les told her. "You ready for another water, little miss?"

"Yes please, and maybe ... if you have that Ovaltine... It might not be so yucky now, if Mister Westley likes it?"

"I do," I lied, "but from now on, you can call me Wes."

"What about 'Dad'?"

My head swam. "Miss Mary, you can call me anything but that. I haven't earned that title."

Les gave me a long look, and Mary slid off my lap to the floor by Raider. Lester stirred her drink, then handed it to her. She mumbled something so softly I couldn't make it out. Raider started licking her ear and the back of her neck in response. She spilled her drink as she tried to hug the life out of my dog. I saw she too had something in her eyes as the tears rolled down her face. Couldn't I do anything right? Was I doomed to try to do the right thing and always have things go sideways? Like Jessica, I'd killed Mary's father as well. Not happy thoughts to have on such a grim morning.

"Is this where all the hootenanny is takin' place?" Grandma said, walking into the kitchen.

"I don't know about all that, Missus Flagg, but—"

"Wes," Grandma said, giving me a warm smile, and plopping down on the stool next to Les.

"Morning, Grandma," I said, then watched, my mouth agape, as she stole my coffee cup and downed it in one swallow.

"I... Grandma, I mean..."

116

"It's one of those mornings," Grandma said, a smile cracking her pretend scowl, "and we have to talk about running off those sumbitches who're pouring into the area."

"Normally I would agree," Grandpa said, walking into the room, rubbing his eyes, "but I can't find my ... son of a—" He grabbed the flask and upended it over his mouth. Only a drop fell out onto his tongue. "Figures," he said, giving me and Les the hairy eyeball.

"Wasn't me, didn't do it. Wouldn't be prudent," I said in my best Bush accent.

Grandma belched. Raider looked up at us and barked while Mary broke out into giggles.

Since I pretty much agreed with what Les had been saying, I busied myself with learning his defenses and meeting the rest of the people who lived on his property. It soon became apparent that I had a hard time remembering new names, but I could recognize faces. There were so many Mikes that I mentally started assigning them numbers. Deputy Rolston walked with me most of the time.

"I know it's asking a lot, but talking it over with my uncle—"

"It's up to Grandpa and Grandma," I told him. "I've tried lone wolfing it a time or two and didn't like what I learned."

Raider barked at that. He'd disappeared for a while, but I'd seen him with Mary on the porch while her mother tried to get her to drink more Ovaltine. Turned out, it was just as gross as I recalled it being.

She'd barely finished the small glass that Les had made her.

"I'm glad," he said, "on both counts—you not minding and that you're ok. What happened?"

"Lance's original crew was taken over by what I thought were some bikers he knew. Turned out they had Marshall hostage elsewhere. When I found out that they were kidnapping women and children, I went for help. I was turned down, so I did it alone. Got a bullet in the shoulder and a cracked skull for my troubles."

Rolston touched his forehead in the corresponding spot to where I'd been stapled, glued, and stitched shut. I nodded.

"You shouldn't be up and about, should you?" he asked.

"Can't slow down, can't stop," I told him. "Those guys were linked up with Henry from Jessica's group."

This had been the first chance I'd had to fill him in on things. The look on his face was shock.

"Her family wasn't involved, and neither were some core members. Right after I tried to break out and Mary got shot, the rest of the group moving south attacked. Henry must have signaled them. It was a slaughter. Jessica and her mom got away with us."

"What happened to her dad?"

I remained quiet for a long moment, then said, "He tried to shoot Raider."

My pup ran in front of me, almost tripping me up. I got my bearings and used the distraction to reach down and roughly push him and pick up a stick. He went very still then his hind end started bunching up. I turned and threw it hard. He took off like a cannonball that had just been lobbed. We watched him for a long second before Rolston turned back to me.

"You killed him?"

"Yeah." I left out the part where I'd also shot my now ex-girlfriend in the face.

"Sorry, that's rough. Sometimes people suck. The purest love out there is what a dog has for his owners," Rolston said quietly.

"We don't own them," I told him as Raider ran over and dropped the stick into my hand. "They own us." I chucked it again, harder this time.

LESTER'S DEFENSES WERE A LITTLE AWE-INSPIRING. ONE of the groups that had been here with him had an IED man during one of the many conflicts in the Middle East, and had seen many countries, and defused a ton of bombs, and I was going to pick his brain on things. What he'd done was set up twelve fougasse cannons. Old steel well casing pipe worked as the barrel. Most were filled with black powder that Lester had from his reloading days, then a wadding and other various things. Some were packed with rocks, old bolts, and ball bearings. Others had lengths of chain and old scrap metal that Les had scavenged from his tumbled barn.

A lot of these defenses could be dug up and moved, I was told, but over and over, I told them to talk to my grandparents. I was just the grandson they'd taken in and raised. I had no legal claim to the homestead, other than calling it home.

Emily, it seemed, was staying away from me today. I was a little grateful, because I was hurt and raw from everything. It wasn't her fault, but I had started feeling like a tug of rope. Little Mary and Emily had been sweet on me in each of their own ways, but I was warring with my own feelings. It wasn't that I didn't care, I did. And that was what scared me.

I'd felt the stirrings of attraction back in the bunker; I recognized that for myself. It was the honest and earnest way she'd been an open book with me. I knew crazy situations sometimes made people feel different about others than they normally would, I remembered that from the movie *Speed*. Emily wore her heart on her sleeve, and Mary was looking for a male figure who didn't scare her to death; they seemed to genuinely like me. But why me? I'd killed, I'd even been the one to kill her father, though I wasn't sure I could share that with her.

I came to a realization all at once and sat under a tree, shelled acorns crunching under my ass. Raider came up, gave me a lick on the face and flopped, then rolled on his back, all four legs kicking his feet skyward, scratching his back in doggy happiness. He was focusing on the moment and letting the rest go, just like I should've done. I'd been so focused on why I was such a horrible human being, I'd ignored the opinions of those around me who thought I was a decent guy, even little Mary who had every reason in the world to dislike me.

I wasn't a bad guy at all. I was a guy who'd seen something impossibly horrible coming and had done my best to make sure those I cared for, was responsible for and loved didn't get hurt. I'd had to do what I'd done, even looking back I really couldn't see any action that could have given me the same results without the same consequences. Of everything that had and could have happened, I'd kept the worst from happening.

"Penny for your thoughts," Grandma said, surprising me and sitting, putting her back against the same tree.

"You'd barely have pocket change," I told her.

"I doubt that. You get the talk from Les and the others?" she asked.

"About wanting to relocate to the homestead?"

Grandma nodded.

"I don't know what to think. It sounds logical, makes sense."

"What do you think, though?" Grandma asked me.

"Probably we should take them up on it. Just the three of us? I don't know. We're pretty tough, us Flaggs, but if they come at us in numbers, or with better equipment..." My voice trailed off as I imagined every horrible scenario.

"Maybe they won't come after us, but I had a

chance to talk to your other girlfriend after you'd left, and I sent Raider to find you—"

"Emily is not—"

She cut me off the same way I had her. "That woman is smitten with you. She knows you're in a pickle right now, and she's willing to wait to see if she's got a chance, but that's not what I was talking about. To her, it sounded like they were interested in testing you. Seeing if you could make drugs and things like that for them."

"Yeah?" I said, confused.

"Well, maybe it isn't just the medical kind they wanted you to make." She pulled a few strands of tall grass, the seed pods heavy.

"I'm pretty sure Henry would have had me cooking meth and speed up if he'd had the chemicals to do it."

"See, and why do you think these private military guys hooked up with him and Lance's group?"

"They wanted something."

"Bingo. Now what would that be?" she asked pointedly.

I wasn't sure, I started to answer, then stopped. The pharmacist had been killed, his private stashes had been stolen, I was sure, along with his store getting emptied. Duke had been the closest thing to a medical doctor there, though Carter was probably a close second. Dead, they were probably both dead. So what would they want? Food? They were getting that here and there, but if they were moving from the more populated areas south, they had to be clearing the countryside like locusts as they went. In all probability, they were good now that they had the food storage of Henry's group for a time. So if it wasn't food, equipment—

"Hey, dummy, you still awake?"

I chuckled as Raider rolled onto his stomach to let his hind leg come up and scratch his ear.

"I'm awake, just thinking. If it's not food, not traditional medicine, what would they want?"

"Drugs, alcohol, women?"

"Why would they leave us alone?" I asked her.

"What if they could trade with us for two of the three?"

I opened my mouth and shut it, then opened it and shut it again, almost sputtering.

"It's easier to make fair trade than kidnap, house, feed and set watch over somebody who's going to do it unwillingly. They would have to worry about what you did to things that might poison them. Obviously, we won't be providing brothel services but..."

"Grandma..." I said shocked.

"Just a thought. I've thought about my garden and the farmer's market a bit and wondered what kind of things people want, what they need, and what will make life more bearable for them. I expect most decent people will be running out of food soon, but we don't want to do that, we're not sure we're self-reliant beyond what you put up."

"I... Grandma... I don't—"

"And I've still got my seeds," she said with a grin, "my garden seeds and other stuff."

"Other stuff?" I asked her.

"Oh, poppies and the stuff that people like for left-handed cigarettes."

I burst into laughter. Grandma was at least a master gardener with decades of experience. She grew food and composted out of necessity. We'd always been poor, but we hadn't gone hungry often. I remembered the lean times, the poaching, and realized that the current timeframe might be something along the same lines.

"You used to grow pot?" I asked her, still laughing.

Raider gave us both a doggy grin and then rolled on his back again, feet kicking. I had to get him a flea collar or something.

"Yeah, never used it myself, but your mom liked to sneak back and help herself. I sometimes wonder if that's how she got started with everything else." Her voice had gone quiet.

"Grandma, you know I've tried it myself, right?" I asked her, hoping my admission would turn the conversation away from the road it was headed.

"Oh, Wes, I knew the first time. There's a distinct smell you can't get out of your clothing, hair, or breath. You didn't do it much."

"Because moonshine was easier to filch," I said with a grin. "Where did you used to grow it?" I asked her, still shocked I didn't know about this.

"Back of our acreage in the low swampy spot.

Didn't have to carry water. I quit about the time you were getting old enough to know what it was, but I kept seeds."

"That old wooden cigar box of seeds you never let me touch?" I remembered finding it in the barn once and asking, only to have the box disappear after that.

"That's the one. Anyway, the idea of giving those guys what they want on trade... It's just a thought."

"Right now, I think we're on the shoot first, ask questions later list, as far as they go," I told her with a grin.

"I expect so. Look, Emily and Mary are waving at you."

I turned and saw both ladies on Les' wraparound porch, sitting on the steps. Both had their hands up. I gave them a lazy wave, and Mary made a come here gesture. I got up and brushed my pants off. Grandma held out a hand, and I helped her up. Raider rolled to his feet once again and shook himself off. I brushed him off as the three of us walked up.

"How're you doing?" I asked Mary.

"I'm doing pretty good. There's lotsa and lotsa people here, Mister Wes. Will you forget we're here if you see too many people?"

"No," I said, mussing her hair.

Emily was rolling her eyes but smiling at her daughter's question. It was cute, and Raider decided it was time for Mary's attention. He flopped at her feet, making her laugh as he started digging at his ear again with his hind leg.

"I think your dog might have split alliances." Emily was smiling as she said it.

"Raider likes the ladies, that's all," Grandma said and walked into Les' house and started shouting for Grandpa.

"So we're going back to your place?" Emily asked me after a long pause.

"I think so. If Grandpa doesn't object."

"Somehow I don't think he will," she told me, looking inside.

13

GRANDPA EXPLAINED what he'd come up with while I'd been outside. Over half of the group was going to be moving today. We didn't have enough vehicles to do it all at once anyway. The first half would be my family, Emily and Mary, and half of the men who had camped out at Les'. Les himself was going to stay until tomorrow and 'supervise' the moving of the traps and cannons. I shuddered to think what those cannons would do to flesh, but I had some ideas of what the one loaded with chains would be good for. Nefarious ideas, the kind that ruined somebody's day most painfully.

Lester's Suburban was packed, and little Mary had to ride on my lap. Grandpa offered to let Emily sit on his, but Grandma had smacked him upside the head for the suggestion. Mary thought that was funny, but her throat was sore today from all the talking. We were following a pickup truck full of men, with Rolston and the sheriff in the bed in front of us. Rifle barrels stuck out all over the place like the quills of a porcupine. Despite the manpower and firepower, I was nervous.

If we were hit from ambush, things could get ugly.

"Wes," Mary asked as we bumped along the dirt road, "where are me and Mom going to stay?"

"With us," I told her.

She leaned back into my chest, her arms wrapped around her stomach.

"Will I have my own room?"

"I don't think any of us are going to have our own rooms, honey," Emily told her.

Raider was laying across Emily and Grandpa's lap in the middle row with us. He wanted to sit upright, but Emily kept pushing his head down, so he didn't squish them both. Getting him in had been a chore.

"If you want, I can take the couch, so you and your mom can have my room," I told her.

Grandma sneezed behind me, but it suspiciously sounded like something else. Grandpa cackled, confirming that it had indeed been more than a cough.

"But you won't fit on a couch. You're super tall." The little girl was observant, but I'd slept on that couch almost as often as my bed over the years.

I'd often sit with the TV, rabbit ears tuned into Saturday cartoons when we got good reception, for as long as my grandparents would allow, often falling asleep with my elbows propping me up, my head in my hands. Part of me was sad that Mary might never have another Saturday like that. It made me wonder how long this was going to last, or if it would never end. I had read that the parts needed to rebuild things in this sort of event weren't manufactured in America. I was desperate for news, information. Being in a news blackout really made me uncomfortable.

"I'll manage," I told her. "Hey, pipsqueak, don't talk so much, you don't want to hurt your throat more, right?"

"How will I know if I'm better if I don't try?" she asked quietly.

"Oh look," Grandma said, pointing over my shoulder. "Foghorn is waiting for us."

Les pulled his Suburban into the drive, sending Grandma's flock of chickens scattering. Raider perked up when he heard the chooks swearing in their fowl language. The first truck pulled in next to the barn, and we stopped next to the house. Les got out first and opened the back door for Grandpa. Raider immediately tried turning around, standing finally. Emily got a dog butt in the face as he took off. I grinned as she sputtered, and Grandpa complained about the dog hitting him in the nads. Grandma was grinning right up until I leaned out the window.

"Go get that rooster!"

Raider took off at a run, his feet kicking up dirt and dust as Foghorn put his wings out, making himself look bigger. My pup didn't slow, so he tucked his wings and took off, making a distressed sound. Grandma smacked me on the back of the head, almost sending me nose first into Mary who was sliding off to get out with her mom.

"Owwwww," I complained.

"If he hurts my baby..." She shook a fist under my nose.

"He won't, it's a game," I said opening my door now I didn't have the beanpole on me.

"Some game," she huffed, letting me get out and then allowing me to help her from the back seat.

"I've missed this place," Grandma told me, looking around.

"I have too. It's been a while for me," I admitted.

"Let's go in, I'll get some coffee going. Can you manage to pump and carry some water?"

I'd been recovering myself, but I'd been stronger day by day. I'd thought that giving blood would have taken more out of me, but I'd bounced back from that quick. Duke must not have drawn out as much as he'd thought, if he was thinking I had been that close to the edge. Even smart people get it wrong sometimes.

"Wait," the sheriff said, walking up. "Let our guys go through the house and barns first, make sure nobody is here—"

I opened the door and whistled. Raider abandoned the chase and came running, his butt wiggling as he saw the open door that led to the kitchen and inside. He cleared the stairs on the porch and was halfway into the house before his feet even touched. I watched as he slid halfway down the hallway before he got himself stopped. He took off sniffing everything.

"Or we could do that," Rolston said, grinning.

"Now, I don't know how many of ya cops are with

this group," Grandpa said, his ornery voice coming out slow, "but there ain't no law now, and if you'll be staying with us, you're going to be looking away while we do our normal bit."

"What's that?" Rolston asked with a grin.

"The usual, making shine, me chasing Grandma around in her bloomers with a can of Redi-Whip."

Grandma cackled as the sheriff's face turned beet red. I'd been used to this kind of banter growing up, but it was still funny, and everyone within earshot either laughed, turned red in the face, or looked away.

"You can make... I mean..." one of the younger guys began; I remembered him as being former military and working with the state police before the balloon had gone up.

"And my grandson here makes a pretty mean rum. If the lights suddenly come back on and the law returns to normal, this shit won't be held against me, you hear?" Grandpa pointed at the men who'd gathered around the porch.

"Aw shit," one of the other guys said. "I'm not going to tell. It's probably your shine I've drank by the gallon over the years, but now I know where it's made, I can cut out the middleman." He was grinning and pointing to Les.

In a masterful moment of maturity, Les adjusted his glasses with his middle finger.

"Can I go inside and use the restroom?" Mary asked her mother.

Emily looked at me, so I turned and whistled.

Raider came bounding from the end of the hall where my bedroom was. His tongue was hanging out in a doggy smile.

"I think it's clear," I told them. "Come on."

"I'm going back for supplies and more men," Les said shortly, "but if you'll save me a jar to sip on, I'd greatly appreciate it."

"You got it," I told him. "Les, thank you."

"I think, son, it's you I should be thanking. For many things." His words trailed off as he looked up the hill, and with a start I realized it was where we'd buried the men who'd chased him.

"Be safe," Grandpa said, "and make sure you bring all the playing cards and coins you can scrounge up."

"Coins?" Les asked surprised.

"We have to have something to gamble with, even if the money's worthless," Grandma shot back.

"Or you and I could play some strip poker," Grandpa cooed.

"Ewwwwwwwwwwww, gross," Mary said from the bathroom she'd just spied, closing the door behind her.

"Little ears," Grandma said, and Grandpa dodged the whack to the back of the head.

THE NEXT WEEK WAS SPENT TRANSPORTING PEOPLE, materials, and defenses they'd built at Lester's to the homestead. The extra hands were given shovels and hoes. Mary helped me direct as we first weeded the big garden Grandma put in for us and watered everything. Then we started double digging the area where the market garden used to be. Double digging was an easy process. You dug a line, leaving the sod, weeds, whatever on the side of the first row. Then you dug a row out, turning everything upside down. It took ten of us half a day to get the old market garden double dug, using the shovels as chisels on some of the harder packed dirt to break things up. We could have used the tractor, but I'd been worried about fuel. We could run it on shine, but with this many people standing around getting bored, we decided to use the labor and do what we could. Some of the potatoes that Grandma and I had stored were going to get re-planted, and we hoped to get a short crop in before winter hit. We'd never done it before, so I was reluctant to try this on a huge scale.

The group worked around the clock, putting the fougasse cannons up along the driveway, on the hillside across the street, and down the road. I'd thought that they had fuses lit by a match, but instead, there was a complicated looking board with buttons and switches, that looked like somebody had raided an auto parts store. A couple of batteries had been linked up to potentially send power to set off the charges, and wires snaked everywhere in the tall grass in the front yard facing the road.

In all this time, I was waiting for Henry to retaliate, for the Crater crew to regroup, for word from Jessica. I realized that was a little self-centered. We'd been working like little bees and I was expecting them to come my way. That wasn't how it was probably going to happen.

"Hey Grandson," Grandpa said, walking up. "What you doing lollygagging about?"

"Sorry," I told him, turning to see the entire yard busy with activity, "I was just thinking about how much we don't know about what's going on in the area, the state and the country. We need a better way to communicate news."

"Already feeling the withdrawal of the global society, made close by the vestiges of the Internet?"

"Vestiges? Grandpa, did you just swallow a thesaurus?"

"Just messing with you. Fancy words out of one of Grandma's magazines. Heh, thought it sounded appropriate."

"It actually is," I admitted, "and in a way, you're right. As a society, we've become complacent about instantaneous information. When I was a kid, if we didn't have the answers here, I'd go to the school library and look it up in an encyclopedia. Nowadays, there's Wikipedia."

"Now yer talking like a dunderhead just like those folks in the magazine," Grandpa said, thumping me on the shoulder.

"Sorry," I grinned and noticed he'd snuck his flask out of the farmhouse.

I snagged it out of the top pocket of his bibs and

took a quick pull before he started to protest. I screwed the cap back on and handed it to him.

"You know, there's bound to be some problems sooner or later."

"Don't I know it," I told him. "What are you worried about specifically?"

"Mostly things having to do with there not being enough wimmin' for all the single guys, not enough booze to smooth over hurt feelings, feeling like we're being watched from all sides."

I shivered; if Grandpa felt like we were being watched, we probably were. He'd honed his senses thanks to a lifetime of lawbreaking and poaching. His instincts had kept him one or two steps ahead of the law more years than I was alive. The rest—the head count of the ladies and booze— was something else he'd probably thrown in to be funny. I hoped.

"Well, I know how to make booze and I need to get stuff out so I can start firing up a small production—"

"Oh, I figured you would, but what if the people see what we've stored? Will they want all the extra that you've worked so hard to put up?"

"I don't know," I admitted. "But I think if we don't find us some piglets to fatten up, we'll have some fermented grains to hand out to people."

Grandma made a pucker face but was nodding. "Sheriff says he's got men doing reconnaissance, those fellas with military experience. They know what they're dealing with, at least as much as we do."

"Good, I sort of like not being the one to point and

direct anymore." Things were sort of falling into a rhythm of their own, people doing what needed doing, now that they were familiar and didn't need hand holding.

A lot of the barn had been cleaned out of the old scrap and junk. It had been carefully stacked behind the barn in piles that made a lot more sense than the way it had been. Grandpa had directed some of the men in what he wanted done with it, but they had gone ahead of that and what they came up with was somewhat startling. Many of the houses they came from had a set of bunk beds for kids they were raising or had been raising. Rows of mismatched bunkbeds and mattresses lined one half of the barn. Old tin and sheets of scrap metal had been tacked to the inside of the barn walls to cut down on the wind blowing straight in. If they wanted better airflow, they cracked one of the doors.

A makeshift outhouse had been constructed for either sex as well, but it was midway back of the property. I was a bit worried about all the comings and goings as vehicles started showing up. Like I'd done with my truck, some of the folks worried about the government taking what was theirs had disabled the vehicles while the sweep was going on. We had close to ten vehicles at any given moment coming, going, or parked. I didn't know where they were getting the fuel, but we weren't providing the moonshine.

"It's good that the young deputy and the sheriff are handling that part," Grandpa said after a long pause.

"You know, I was thinking," I started to say, but Grandpa interrupted.

"There you go, thinking again..." he mock groaned.

"One of the things I didn't prep for was sanitation on a larger scale. Some of these folks are taking spit baths with a bucket out back when they can. What if I put one of the water barrels up on a platform and put a spigot in the bottom with a shower head or something... Paint the barrel black so people can take warm showers? And soap, we don't have enough for everybody."

"I'm ok with that project, but what are we going to do about soap?"

"We can make some. It's not that hard."

"Your grandma knows how to do that pretty good actually. Used to sell it when you were little. She's got wooden molds in the attic somewhere."

"Do we have any lye?" I asked.

"If we can't find some, I know how to make it with wood ashes," Grandpa told me. "You worried the smell of body odor will give us away?" He was grinning easy, his lips pulled back, showing his teeth.

"Well, it'd certainly help there, but..." I looked up as Raider ran to us from the house, barking happily, "More along the lines of keeping disease and infection down. Without modern conveniences, we're living like it's the 1800s again."

"I ought to slap ya," Grandpa said with a grin. "Thirty years ago we were living like this when times were hard."

"Well then, maybe I should put you in charge of the projects," I shot back.

"Maybe I should be in charge then!"

"Good, it's decided," I told him, petting my dog.

Grandpa grunted then turned. I followed him back toward the house where Grandma was showing Emily and several of the ladies who'd come with the group how to wash in an old tub, her antique washboard put to use once again. Suds were everywhere and Mary was happily blowing bubbles from a bubble stick she'd found somewhere with the soapy water. I was pretty sure they were using dish soap, but I wasn't sure.

"What's for dinner tonight?" I asked Grandma as I walked up.

"Go hunt something up," Grandma said. "I've been talking to the people here, and nobody's been having enough protein unless it's been tinned meat."

"I ... ok," I told her, sort of surprised.

Grandma had had her canner going as some of the garden had been harvested earlier in the year, and she often canned the meat when we had extra, we didn't want to put in the fridge. That was still under the coop though, still hiding our food storage. We'd been eating normally though. Cornbread was made on the fireplace, even though it heated up the house, and a simple beans and rice mixed with lentils had started creeping into the lunch and suppertime meals. Breakfast was still good old eggs with cornbread though.

"You want to take one of the guys with you?" Grandma asked.

"No," I told her, "You know how it is when I'm hunting. If it isn't Grandpa—"

"Then they walk like they've got two left feet, playing trumpets and trombones."

"Exactly," I said. "Going to get my rifle out of your room."

"You going hunting, Mr. Wes?" Mary asked me.

"Looks like it, kiddo. What you want me to get you?" I asked.

"I want a big mac and a Coke!" she said, laughing as everyone stopped what they were doing and let out a moan of wanting.

"How about a fat rabbit or two, or a deer if I can stalk one down?"

"That'd be great!" she said with a grin.

The ladies looked at me strangely, knowing each family was on their own for food. I couldn't tell if it was jealousy or not. One of the rules that the men had enacted was that very few would go trampling around in the woods. It was more to keep them safe while the guys patrolled. They were worried about friendly fire at worst, or a heart attack as somebody ghosted out of the darkness at the least.

"When we get back, we can use my old enamel canner and make a pretty good stew," Grandma said, "it should be enough to get everyone a small bowl full at least?"

There were whispers from the ladies, a grin from Mary, and Emily just beamed a big smile at me.

"I'm going to get my box of snare material from my

closet too," I told Grandma, more so to let Emily know I was going into the room her and Mary had been using.

"Need a hand?" Emily asked, standing and brushing her soapy hands on her jeans.

"I'm good," I told her, "should be on the top shelf in a shoebox."

"Ok, bring us back something delicious."

"Yes, ma'am," I told her.

I walked inside, collecting the silenced .22-250 and a handful of cartridges and shoving them in my pocket, then headed into my bedroom. Emily's touch was everywhere. She'd straightened things out and had picked wild flowers to put on the dresser. She and Mary didn't have much in the way of clothing for themselves, and they kept their belongings in a box Grandpa had found for them somewhere. She was trying to leave minimal impact on my space, I was sure, but I didn't mind the couch. Other than the fact Raider had been waking me up by doing a patrol of the house, then trying to lay on top of me off and on in the middle of the night.

My pup followed me around, and I grabbed my camo netting, stuffing it into my backpack along with my canteen. I looked at the M4 I had taken off the dead man and considered using that instead. The handloads for the .22-250 were few, but Grandpa and Lester could reload more, plus the M4 wasn't suppressed. Last to put in was my box that held my snare kit. I took that to the kitchen table and sat down. Les was there, drinking a cup of tea, watching me.

"You going head hunting?" he asked as I opened the box.

"No, just going to see if I can get some meat to start a big pot of stew," I told him pulling out some wire and some copper fittings.

"Looks like you're going to be setting out some snares too. You ever do that for uh..." He looked around to see was in earshot, old habit, "bigger game?"

"Yeah," I told him, grinning. "Usually set my deer snares up a little higher and tie the wire off on a log to use as a drag. That way the deer doesn't bang itself up too much as it's dying."

"That what you're making right now?" he asked as I pulled a good seven feet of wire out of a spool I'd had wrapped tight.

"Yeah, I'm going to use a camlock for this one. Rabbits don't usually need it, but a deer snare... the deer sometimes break the wire. With a camlock, it tightens around their neck and if it breaks, it's usually after the camlock, so they still die. Ruins the snare, but they usually aren't any good anyways. Still find the deer though."

Les grunted and took a sip as I quickly made two big snares like I'd described. He watched, fascinated. I took some snares I'd already made up a while back that had a smaller length of wire I'd used for small game trapping. I hoped I didn't get a skunk again, that really, excuse the term, stank, when that happened. I put half a dozen in my bag and then closed the box up.

"Be safe, Wes."

"You too," I told him, "Raider, you stay and make sure the old man doesn't get into my rum."

Raider let out a low bark in agreement, sitting down, his entire butt wiggling, while Les shot me the finger.

14

LESTER HAD RADIOED the crew that I was headed out to go hunting for some supper, so nobody got itchy on their trigger fingers. I'd changed into my wool poacher's garb, hot and scratchy, but oh so quiet, and headed out, my pack lighter than it usually was. I had an idea about going across the street to the Crater. I wanted to see if everyone had cleared out like I'd been told, but more than that, the fields that were usually plowed for gem hunters, were now a lush grass that was probably close to a good four feet tall in spots. Half of it had been burned in the fires I'd caused, but I was banking on new growth.

New growth seemed to be what critters craved. Probably sweeter tasting and chocked full of nutrition they'd be hard pressed to find elsewhere. I heard a low whistle to my left as I was crossing the road and saw one of the deputies wave to me from behind what looked like a ground blind. I walked over, waving until I was positive he could tell it was me.

"Hey, Wes," Deputy Stevenson said. "Got the message you're headed out hunting. What time should we expect you back?"

"Unless I bag something big right away, I'll probably set some traps out and wait until dusk and be back after dark."

"Ok, I'm here until about 1900," he said, "but I'll let my replacement know."

"Sounds good," I told him quietly, looking up the hill. "Take it easy."

"Be safe," he said, echoing the statement that had been said to me multiple times already.

I gave him a curt wave and took off as he got into his position again, pulling a camo tarp back in place, giving him some cover as well as keeping direct sunlight off him. I grinned as I started walking. It wasn't a horrible way to hunt, but I'd learned how to stalk deer and move quietly as a kid. When I set out for meat, I'd get it if there was some out there to be had in the area. It was a skillset learned out of necessity and one I hoped would put some smiles on everybody's faces.

Behind me, the distinctive sound of the tractor firing up caught my attention, but I didn't let it slow me down. Grandpa was doing something, and I wasn't going back to check. I put on my hat with the mosquito face netting when I was almost to the top of the ridge of the caldera and stopped, setting my rifle against a tree.

I reached into the leaves, pushing and pulling them away until I got to the rocky rich soil beneath. I scraped some of it up, the leaves having held in the moisture, and rubbed the soil on the tops of my hands, darkening them with the dirt and covering up my scent. Then I rubbed the leaves across the front of my wool suit and under the arms. It wasn't going to do much to cover my scent, but if it gave me an extra half a second of indecision when a deer might have scented me, it would be worth it. Old habits die hard.

Then I started the stalk.

THE SOUTHERN PORTION OF THE FIELD WHERE I USED TO prospect for diamonds was thick with growth, and I could see where people or larger animals had made trails through the tall grass. I'd find spots at the edge of the woods to set my snares, but I first wanted to see the wreckage I'd caused and see if anybody was still about. I worked my way carefully in the fading afternoon light until I was within eyesight of the wreckage. Where the fires had burned, there was new growth of grass and weeds, as I expected. A few burned out cars and several motorcycles were left in place, along with three burned out trailers.

Deep ruts behind the welcome center showed that more than a few trucks had gotten stuck while trying to pull their rigs out of there. As far as people? I saw no evidence. I worked my way to the station where the hand pump was, to where the water sluices were set up. The grass was still tall here around it, but the concrete pad gave me a spot in the middle of the greenery to sit down and make sure I was alone out here. I took my pack off and used the rifle's scope to look around me. I didn't know if the roving patrols had checked over this area, but I wished I had now.

It'd be helpful to know who was about, how long it'd taken them to bug out, and if they'd come back in to strip parts off the vehicles left behind. All information I didn't know. Jessica's group had known, and with a start, I realized why they hadn't wanted to jump into my rescue mission. Henry had probably given them a BS reason, but all along he'd been working with them. My hatred for the man grew a notch. It hadn't made any sense to me at the time that Jessica and her parents weren't in on saving the women and children when they'd already gone it to help the Gutheries out.

The Gutheries, the baker and her husband. My friends. I realized in the insanity that'd happened at the bunker and the subsequent shootings, I had no idea what had happened to them. Had they been a part of Henry's plan? I doubted it. Had they been executed like the rest of the people who weren't in on Henry's plan? Probably.

My heart heavy, I almost missed the flicker of movement at the edge of the new growth about two hundred feet in front of me. It was an ear flickering just above the tall grass. I made a low sound that sounded like a lamb going baaaaa. A head snapped up right where I thought it might be. I didn't see spots on the neck as the deer looked around. Another deer huffed from somewhere up ahead from another direction.

I flipped the safety off, and slowly squeezed the trigger, taking up slack and let my breath out slowly. My entire focus narrowed, my heartbeat seemed to slow. The deer turned so it was facing away from me again when I sent the lead down target. The suppressed gun made about as much noise as I remembered, but I could hear the subsonic .22-250 hit the target, just behind the eye, with a 'thwap' sound.

"One down," I said, taking my pack off, taking my eyes off the target for a moment.

This had been too easy. I never killed anything this quickly. I stowed my pack under the bench and made sure I had my belt knife handy while I reloaded and did a slow count to three hundred. When I got to it, I kept scanning the area. I hadn't seen the deer get up or move, which I was pretty sure was impossible with part of its skull missing and its brain mushed.

I stood slowly, using my scope to see if anything or anybody had heard the shot. I didn't see any movement, but I knew there was at least one other deer out here. It'd blown a warning to others from somewhere off to my left as I'd been sighting in on the one I'd just downed. It might have slunk off as soon as it'd seen or smelled something off, but if I got a chance to bag two, I was positive I could get help hauling them out. I'd gotten doubles before, not often, but it'd happened enough that I crept up on the downed deer as if I was still hunting.

My boots made little sound, but the rifle banged against my back as I'd slung it crossways across my back. I could live with it. I just made sure to put the strap around my good shoulder. The night was silent, and I heard the deer blow again. I paused and rose up a little bit above the grass to see if I could see it standing out. I made it quick, then put my head down and made the rest of my way on all fours. The doe was within a couple feet of where I'd shot her. She must have had one last impulse to leap or move as her body was shutting down, but she didn't get far.

I started the process of butchering her by bleeding her out, before gutting her. When that was done, I looked at the organs. The world was different. Grandpa loved heart meat, Grandma liver, but I knew the Native Americans used more than that. I sighed and pulled a plastic bag out of my pocket and put those in before doing the zip seal up. What was the world going to be like, when all the Ziplocs were gone? I stuffed the organ meat in my deep pockets then started pulling grass out. I soaked up as much of the moisture out of the cavity as possible, then hoisted the deer over my shoulders.

When poaching, dragging a deer out might be easier all around, but it left drag marks, blood, and hair. When you wanted to stay ahead of the law, you do what I did. I hoisted the deer onto my shoulders in a fireman's carry, the head flopping off my right as I held onto the front and back legs with my hands. It was a nice doe, one who'd probably already dropped babies this past spring. They should be weaned by now, so I didn't feel horrible about taking her.

The disadvantage of carrying a deer the way I was? Besides the fact I'd have to wear my backpack and gun the wrong way? I wouldn't be able to sneak as effectively. I was wary of that fact, even though I was pretty sure the possum sheriffs wouldn't be out in force. Predators of the two and four-legged variety might be about, and I kept scanning ahead of me as I got to the sluice station. I hoisted the deer over my shoulders with the intent of putting it on the dried out sluice station when something seemed to push the deer, sending me off balance and off my feet.

I fell hard, the deer hitting the waist-high water table. My bad shoulder flared out in agony and I laid there a moment, biting my cheek so as not to cry out. I checked the rifle, making sure I hadn't bent the barrel or plugged it up. I'd scuffed the wood on it, but that was all. What had caused me to go off balance? I'd heard something, but I was so surprised by being knocked off my feet that I wasn't sure. I crawled to the table and looked at the deer, intending to see how badly I might have bruised up the meat. What I saw made me suck in a breath of shock.

The shoulder had been pulverized, but not from the fall. A fresh bullet hole was in the carcass. I dropped to the floor, ignoring the pain again. Somebody had taken a shot at me from afar. I hadn't even heard the buzzing sound of a bullet, but if I was right, they had been aiming at my head and had fired the same instant I'd lifted the deer to put it down.

I broke into a cold sweat and crawled to my backpack. I pulled out the handheld radio that Jess had given me a long time back. I had a couple of the frequencies programmed that the guys were using at the homestead. I was pretty sure I could reach them from here, but these worked on a line of sight usually. I keyed up.

"Silent hunter, anybody see any possum sheriffs in the area? Over."

I knew if Grandpa was listening, he'd answer, or somebody who recognized my voice might get him to a radio. I repeated the call and waited.

"This is Jed Clampet," Grandpa's voice said out of the radio a few minutes later. "What area you looking at? Over."

I thought about it, how to tell him without quickly giving up my location.

"The place I found the tin for the new roof, over."

There was a long pause, then, "No possum sheriffs reported. What's the hunting like?"

"Hot, and I'm not the only one in the area. Over."

There was cussing on the line before he remembered to speak. "Is the situation because of some ornery birds of prey? Over."

"Think so," I responded, forgetting to say over.

"I've got the big Richard here, he says he can get a team to you to cover your tail. You want him to?"

"If possible, can they do a sweep of the southwest tree line? I've got a long-distance hunter, almost as quiet as me, working the field. If yes, be careful, they have elevation and appear to be a good shot."

It was out now, I could have phrased it differently, but I hadn't thought that one as thoroughly.

The radio beeped and somebody else broke in on the transmission, a familiar voice coming out of the handset.

"Silent Hunter, this is Girl Scout," Jess's voice said. "Wait one hour, then get out of there. You copy? Over."

"Girl Scout and Jed Clampet, Silent Hunter copies message. Please be warned that any approach on my location by unknowns might be mistaken as a competitor poaching on my hunting ground. If they intend to approach my location, give me a shout long before they come into eyesight. Over."

"Message received," Jessica said out of the radio. "Keep your head down, over."

"Will do. Silent Hunter out."

"Copy Message, Jed Clampet out."

I HAD NO INTENTION OF STAYING IN THAT SPOT. I PULLED my backpack to me and took some cordage out, before dragging the deer down on the cement slab with me. I tied both feet together to make it easier when I hefted it onto my shoulders next, then got my drag rope out and put it in my pocket, putting the organ meat in my backpack. I was going to watch what was going on, but this spot wasn't as safe or as ideal as I'd first thought. Not with a sniper shooting from elevation and distance. I left my pack, but took my rifle, binoculars, and radio, and crawled out into the grass, using the wooden beams to hide as much of my body as possible in case somebody tried to lob some lead my way. It was a piss poor backstop, but it gave me time to slowly weave some tall strands of grass through my netting and a chance to look for movement.

I thought about where the shot had come from, and when I was ready, I crawled under the netting, pulling it over me, and crawled ten yards north of where I had been, at the edge of a rocky outcropping. I used that as a rest and put the rifle up and started glassing the tree line. I started at the base of the trees, slowly going back and forth, then started moving up, not focusing on any one thing, but looking for shapes, movement.

The day was growing darker, and I had no idea if the hour had gone by yet, so I turned on the radio, looking at the readout and set it beside me, on low, in case somebody called. I was almost ready to pack things in when a flash of light caught my attention. I focused on it. About twenty feet or more off the ground, I made out a shape. It was fuzzy at first, and no matter how I focused on it, I couldn't make it out. Then

I saw the rifle barrel and scope. My breath caught as the gun pointed my way.

I fired half a second before I saw the muzzle flash. The ground erupted to my right, and I rolled, not caring that I was disturbing a swath of grass putting the outcropping between me and the shooter. Unless I stuck my head up, I'd be out of sight. Without looking, I reached for the radio, pawing at the ground until I found it.

"Silent Hunter here. Unknown poachers on site. Unless otherwise directed, engagement of hostile poacher is unavoidable. They are treed and unable to move at this time."

"Silent Hunter, no unknown poachers from our hunting party are in that location yet," Grandpa's voice came through with a nervous edge.

"About to get hot here," I said as another round hit the ground far off to my left, where I had been before. "About to confront aggressor."

"We're hurrying, son."

I put the radio down and moved up inch by inch with the rifle, reloading it. I found the tree again quickly and saw where the round had hit the tree and saw the shape climbing down, trying to go slow, in no hurry. They took their shot and were now going to run away? Oh hell no. Not this time. I lined up my shot on center mass of the shape and slowly squeezed the trigger as I exhaled. Half a heartbeat after the lead left the rifle, I lost the picture as the radio erupted my concentration.

"Wes, don't! That's my mom!" Jess's voice said out of the radio, forgetting to use my call sign.

But the round had already been fired, and I glassed the tree again, finding what I was looking for a moment later. A figure was hanging off a low branch and fell to the ground.

"Target down," I said quietly.

I IGNORED the radio as I took off at a dead run toward the tree. I'd shot Linda. I knew now who had been shooting at me, and Jessica's warning had come too late. I wasn't sure what sort of hell I'd just unleashed. I wasn't the only one crashing through the brush. I figured Jessica had been making tracks as well, and I knew Grandpa would have relayed message to the team who was making their way to me. I knew I was being reckless, but maybe Linda had thought I was one of Lance's crew who'd sneaked in?

Too many thoughts, not enough information. I felt like puking as a cold, greasy feeling filled the lower pit of my guts. I'd kept the rifle on me, held in front as I dashed the last hundred feet to the base of the tree. I was scared of what I'd find, but what I found had me stop short. Linda was sitting on the ground, shirtless, a vest sitting in the grass near her. She'd used her under-shirt to press against her bare chest, under her left boob, where a trickle of blood had leaked around the edges.

"Linda—"

"Get out of here," she hissed, using her arm to try to cover her bareness.

"You need help, I—"

"It didn't go all the way through my vest, now get out of here before I kill you."

She had a handgun on the ground near her right side, pointed my way.

"What the hell happened? Did you think I was one of—"

"I knew exactly what I was doing." Her words were cold.

She'd tried to kill me. On purpose. I had the rifle in front of me, but now I brought it up low and approached her. She went very still at the sight of the barrel pointing at her and dropped her shirt, putting her hands up with a wince. I saw the outline of what had to have been a plate in the vest on her left side. It had made an instant bruise. I saw her rifle past the vest, out of reach. Good. I picked up her pistol, her eyes never leaving me, and slung my rifle.

"How bad is it?" I asked her.

"Edge of the plate cut me, or some spalling from the shot." Her hands were in the air, pulling her chest tight. It didn't look bad, I was expecting a bullet hole, but she was right—it was a gash.

"Please, stop the bleeding and cover yourself," I

said, flushing when I realized I was checking out Jessica's mother's um...

"Wes, please, report in." Jessica's voice came out of my radio.

I'd tuned it out mentally, but now I slung the rifle and kept the 1911 in my left hand so I could cover her and talk.

"Your mother's fine. You'd like to explain to me what the hell just happened?"

"Is she hit?" Jessica asked, panic in her voice.

I watched as Linda slowly pulled her shirt on then pressed her hand under her left breast, putting pressure on the gash.

"Plate took the round. She's got a cut, some bruises. You coming this way to collect her, or is my group taking her to the homestead for questioning?"

The old anger was creeping into my voice again. I didn't like it, but I couldn't help it. Linda had been at odds with me ever since the attempted rescue of the women and children, and now she'd gone so far as trying to murder me, by her own words.

"Wes, please wait for me. Mom radioed me her location right before I got back with you... Over."

"She did it on purpose. She was shooting to kill me. Over."

"You don't know that," she said, and in the background, I could hear her panting.

She must have been running, just like I had been. My nerves were on fire, and I had to fight the tunnel vision. I could hear somebody running hard in the distance.

"I'll never forgive you," Linda said, her voice low.

"I'll never forgive myself either," I told her, "but I'll get over it. He was going to kill my dog, and I wasn't aiming at his head."

"You weren't—"

I hadn't been. The angle I'd shot at him, I was hoping for a glancing shot that'd spin him around. He was so close I couldn't have missed. Jess had jumped in the way, the bullet punching through one cheek, hitting a tooth before exiting the other side. I had been solidly aiming for his gun shoulder.

"No, and unfortunately I've now shot all of your family at some point or another," I spat.

A deflected bullet had killed him. The sound of something cracking in the woods and pounding feet was getting louder, but I turned, hearing it coming from behind where I'd been. The cavalry?

"How'd you get the drop on me?" she asked.

"Your scope reflected light at me as I was scanning the trees," I admitted.

"I must admit, I almost didn't see you," Linda said, wincing as she put more pressure on.

"What gave me away?" I asked her.

"A new lump next to the rock I used when setting up my range card," she said, a grimace crossing her features.

"Silent Hunter, got you in sight," a familiar voice said. "Situation?"

"Unfriendly disarmed, her daughter is running to us. Do not fire on her," I said almost as an afterthought. My guts twisted as the thought of Jessica being killed made me feel things I'd been pushing down and as far out of my thoughts as I could.

"Target sighted. She makes a move with her guns, I've got three sets of scopes on her. Over."

"Girl Scout here," a breathless Jessica said into the radio, the sounds of crashing through the woods slowing down. "Coming in. I'll disarm as soon as I'm near Silent. Copy?"

"You better," came the reply out of the radio, and the voice sounded like Rolston.

The guy who'd made me feel a twinge of jealousy when he'd been with the government forces sweeping the area and had mentioned having dinner and wine with her. He was now warning her off. That was the moment Jessica walked into sight, stepping into the immediate area we were at.

"Mom?" Jessica said, her hands still up.

"I think the edge of the plate got me," she said, gasping.

"She's got a gash under her left breast. Plate left a bruise, and she fell out of the tree. Need to check her to see how banged up she is. Your mom is running on hatred and adrenaline right now."

I tried not to look at Jessica, but she was pulling the carbine off her back by the sling, holding it away from her and putting it on the ground near her mother's dropped rifle.

"The pistol too," I told her.

"Wes, I wouldn't shoot—"

"She would, now disarm before you get near her." My words were harsher than I'd intended, and my rifle was pointed between them.

"Wes, I can't believe that—"

"No arguing, missy," a gruff voice said, ghosting out of the woods to the west of us, about twenty feet away.

Jessica let out a groan, then dropped her utility belt. It was one of those reinforced canvas belts that held her holster, belt knife, and magazine pouches. She let it all fall, then held her hands up again, spinning.

"Go ahead," I told her, motioning with the rifle.

A few heads popped up around us as the group from the homestead closed in.

"Hold on, guys," I said, "she's gotta take her mom's shirt off."

I was going to save her some dignity if nothing else.

"What about you?" Linda asked.

"Ain't nothing I haven't already seen, ma'am," I said, my voice almost a growl. "Not taking my eyes off you until you're far out of my sight."

"Mom," Jess said, kneeling and pulling her shirt up, hesitating, then she pulled the white undershirt off.

The shirt was bloody in splotches, like a tie-died shirt that had only had one color from when she'd had it smashed against her skin. Jess looked at me, but I just stood there as Jess pulled her mother's hand away.

She made a sound in her throat, then probed the edge of the bruise, making her mom gasp.

"I can't feel anything broke. If Duke and Carter were here..."

"They're dead," Linda spat.

"I know," she said, pulling her mom forward and then feeling her back along the ribs. I could see she'd have a hell of a bruise at the base of her spine from hitting a branch or the ground when she'd landed.

"You getting an eyeful?" Linda spat at me.

"I've seen more of you than I'd care to," I told her. "This ain't for cheap thrills; you tried to kill me. Haven't decided what to do with you yet."

"You can't do anything," Linda said, pulling her shirt down and putting her right hand over the gash again to stop the trickle of blood.

"In theory, I could do lots of things. I could shoot you right here. I could tie you up and drop you near Henry's people. I can't just let you walk away after trying to kill me."

"You won't do any of that," Linda hissed. "Like I said, you can't do anything."

"No, but I can. Linda and Jessica Carpenter. You're under arrest. You have the right to remain silent," Sheriff Jackson said, and Deputy Rolston walked up, the younger man carrying a single pair of handcuffs in his left hand.

"For what?" Jessica asked, putting her hands up as she realized there were now ten men and women converging on us, guns drawn.

"Attempted murder and whatever else I can think of," Sheriff Jackson said mildly, tossing the cuffs to Jessica.

She glared at him as she cuffed one wrist of hers, then put the other loop on her mom's left hand.

"You boys carry their weapons and packs." It was a command, not a request. "Where's the rest of your kit?" he asked me.

"Back at the water station. I..." The adrenaline was giving me the shakes. "Jessica, where are your dogs?" I asked her.

"With friends," she snapped.

"And I hate to be impolite," Rolston asked me, "but were you able to uh..."

"If somebody wants to help me drag a deer out, we'll have stew and steaks tonight," I told him, noticing everybody grinning.

"Damn deer took the shot meant for your head," Linda said quietly.

"I noticed that," I told her. "You know, if you were a man, I'd..."

"You'd what?" she taunted, her smile almost a sneer.

My fist flew like a whip. She flinched as I stopped it a good foot from her face.

"You're lucky," I said, noting Jessica's shocked face, "that I'm still a gentleman. That I still respect you and have feelings for your daughter, whatever they might be."

In a small voice, Jessica said, "You're not the Westley I used to know."

"A lot has changed," I told her.

"I can't ... this is too much." She started crying.

I went back for my pack, two of the men following me to help carry, or drag, the deer out. This spot was ruined for a while with all the noise and scent left behind.

16

We built a fire between the barn and the chicken coop. When it was going good, Grandma got out an old cast iron tripod set and hung chains with hooks on the end then hooked up a metal grill she'd had stashed in the barn. I'd seen this used before, but it was a long, long time ago when I was a little boy. She had a hard time lifting the nearly full pot, so Emily and one of the other ladies teamed up. The pot itself Grandma called her old enameled canner, but it really looked like a fire-blackened cauldron. We'd butchered the deer near the front porch, throwing scraps to Raider who sat poised to strike like a vulture waiting on nearly dead roadkill to die.

Some steaks we'd cut and set aside in the house, but most of the meat was in the pot. The carrots, potatoes, and onions we'd harvested from our kitchen garden were rinsed off at the well, then roughly chopped and added to the meat before they'd filled the pot with water.

"Next time, maybe we should fill the pot after it's hung on the fire," Emily said, red-faced from the exertion.

"Ya think?" Grandma said, gasping for breath.

I grinned. The ladies had been faster than Grandma could have asked me for help. I had a feeling that the ladies had been on short rations. They were all on the same end of the world diet we all were on, but some of them looked gaunt to almost the point of looking like third world refugees. With a start, I realized it was probably from giving their food portions to their kids and the husbands who were doing all the work.

"I do. Wes, where are we going to stash your girlfriend's mom?" Emily asked me sweetly.

Raider let out a low growl from next to where I'd sat to skin, quarter, and chop potatoes.

"Easy, boy," I said, rubbing his head. "I don't know what they've got in mind for Jessica and Linda Carpenter." I deliberately didn't use the term 'girlfriend'.

"You know, she had no idea her mom was stalking you?" Grandma asked me.

"You talked to her?" I asked, surprised.

"Sure. Asked that hoity-toity bitch why she was trying to hurt my grandson." She punctuated the words with waving a steel ladle about, pointing at the barn.

"I killed her husband," I answered.

"You said yourself, you weren't aiming at his head, you were too close to miss."

"No, the bullet deflected after it took out the back of Jessica's jaw," I answered her softly.

"So you didn't mean to kill him, just stop him from killing one of your family."

The group around us had gone silent.

"Grandma, you realize that now I've shot every single family member of the Carpenters?" I asked her.

"You've been shot yourself, doing the job they should have been doing," Grandma fired back.

I sighed and stretched my legs out. I was sweating from being close to the fire, but it felt good. We'd left some of the larger sections of leg bone in the bottom of the pot and the entire neck to go along with the chunks we'd cut, once we'd removed the windpipe.

"I figured out why they wouldn't," I said, watching as Jessica and Linda were led out of the barn at gunpoint, and in our direction.

"Why's that?" Emily asked.

"Because Henry was working with the guys from the Crater. I thought them getting the Gutheries out of there with a big distraction and nobody really getting hurt was kind of weird."

"Well, it wasn't weird, we're just that good," Linda said as she was pushed onto her butt across the fire from me.

"Henry probably radioed ahead when he realized you guys were going no matter what. He played you.

He played all of us," I said softly, listening to the fire crackle.

Jessica sat between her mother and me, in front of the ladies and kids who were standing around us in a circle. Both of them were handcuffed, but I knew how dangerous Linda was, and I definitely had a good idea Jessica was even better hand to hand. I was glad I was out of range of their legs. Emily abruptly got up and walked away in the direction of the house. I followed her with my eyes as far as I could, the fire having ruined my night vision. Lots of people were going to be staying up late into the night for this feast.

The door to the house banged shut, and Raider let out a low whine.

"I know, boy, she's probably as pissed as the rest of us are."

"Where's her daughter?" Grandma asked.

"Sleeping," I told her. "She conked out on the couch reading one of my old books."

"Are you going to be ok to carry her to bed? I'm not sure I'm steady enough on my feet—"

"I'll take care of it," I assured her.

"Why did you try to kill him?" one of the ladies asked from behind me, somebody who also related to the sheriff, if I remembered correctly.

"He killed my husband," Linda said simply, repeating the words she'd said a few times already.

"You know what he's done here? What he's been trying to do?" The woman to my left stepped forward, and I could see her out of the side of my eye. I recognized her from somewhere.

"The road to hell is paved with good intentions," Linda shot back.

"Mom, shut up," Jessica said, her voice not quite a snarl.

Linda turned to her daughter, shock on her face. "You still love him after all he's done to our family?"

"There's no reason he needs to die because of what happened to Dad, me, and what almost happened to you. There's been enough killing."

The door banged shut, and I turned. In a couple moments, I saw Emily stalking toward us with a box of shells and that monstrous revolver in her hands. Her face a mask of anger and something darker. It was almost the look she'd had when she'd come unhinged. She paused next to me then kicked my left foot. I moved my leg, confused.

She sat in the hollow spot between my legs and leaned against my chest, startling the hell out of me.

"You know what he's done for me?" the woman to my left repeated.

"What?" Linda said, her words sarcastic as she looked at the woman like she'd been an annoying interruption.

"He kept me from getting repeatedly raped, like they'd been doing for the days before he saved me."

Linda flinched, and Jessica looked down then up again, recognition showing in her eyes.

"See, she remembers." She pointed at Jessica, then walked off in a huff.

"I didn't mean..." Linda said, then broke down into sobs.

Emily wiggled, making herself more comfortable, but making me very uncomfortable. We'd been close, but that was sharing warmth. What was she doing here? Marking territory? I wasn't sure this would help, and to be honest, I didn't want to be somebody's trophy to be claimed. My feelings were all in turmoil, and to be honest, Emily sort of scared me.

"See this?" Emily said, opening the back of the large single action revolver, letting the stainless steel gleam in the firelight.

"Yeah," Jessica said, finally looking over at us and realizing how close Emily was sitting to me, if the look on her face was any indication.

"It's a BFR. Stands for Big Framed Revolver, but I call it a big fucking revolver. It takes .30-30 Winchester rounds."

"I've seen it in action," Jessica said.

She loaded one cartridge, then spun the cylinder and loaded another. "Then I want you both to know something. I don't have a whole lot in this world I care about. Like Charity back there," she said, bobbing her head in the direction the woman had gone, "but I have a lot to be thankful for because of this big lug." She loaded another cartridge, spinning the cylinder. "And if something were to happen to him, and either of you were responsible..." Her words fell off as she loaded the fifth cartridge, snapping the catch closed.

Then she raised the pistol in a smooth motion, cocking the big hammer back. Grandma let out a gasp, having heard about Emily's savage side, then grabbed people standing behind Jessica and Linda, pushing them away from where the barrel was aimed.

"If either of you are responsible for him getting hurt again, I'll end you. Do I make myself clear?"

"Yes," Linda said softly, her words almost sobs, her body trembling.

"Everything is clear to me now," Jessica said, her words dripping with venom as she looked between me and Emily.

"Raider, go check on the girl," I told him, not trusting him to stay calm with all this tension and a gun now in play.

Raider sneezed at me, laying belly down on the ground, proving he had more sense than I gave him credit for. I sighed then slid back as Emily jumped up, the gun still pointing at Linda's head from across the fire. I thought she was going to shoot, then she let the hammer down and let the gun hang loosely at her side.

"Ok, I just wanted to make things crystal fucking clear."

We all warily watched her as long as she was in sight. She'd been walking stiffly, the only sounds were the fire and her footfalls, until the door to the house punctuated her exit. The men who had Linda and

Jessica at gunpoint looked shaken, but they stood their ground when the others moved out of the way.

"I think she got her point across rather well," Rolston said, to his uncle, the sheriff, "don't you?"

Sheriff Jackson nodded to his nephew. "Pretty clear to me."

"How many?" Linda asked me.

"How many what?" I responded.

"How many ladies and kids? How many of them here were...?"

"I didn't ask for a count," I told her, "but about half of them, I imagine, since that's how many you freed and then turned loose to fend for themselves. Many families had no idea where their wives, daughters, or kids had been taken."

"We couldn't have known. It's—"

"It's different when it isn't you it's happening to," I told her. "I get that. I can even forgive you for that, if you'd understand where the rest of us are coming from."

"I don't..." Her words trailed off as she started hyperventilating.

"Mom?" Jessica asked, startled, scooting near her mom and checking her pulse. "Slow your breathing."

"I can't, I didn't..."

She leaned into Jessica and blew out a big breath like she'd been holding it in instead of panting like a runaway engine.

"I know, Mom, it's easier when you don't think about it. Slow down, you're going to pass out."

Linda cupped her hands as best she could over her mouth and breathed into them, trying to slow her breathing. I reached into my pocket and pulled out a mostly clean handkerchief and got up and walked to her, holding it out gingerly. She took it and wiped her face, then blew her nose.

"Were any of you there? At the crater?" Her words were for the crowd of people who'd come to surround us.

There were some nods from the people watching this train wreck of a soap opera episode.

"I'm so sorry, I'm so sorry," she sobbed.

Something inside of me broke loose. The anger I'd been feeling was crushed under what felt like a boot putting out a cigarette. I understood at least now. I didn't like it, but I could empathize with it. Something had happened to her, or to Jessica, and she couldn't deal with it, didn't want to deal with it. The horrors had happened after the Gutheries kidnapping, so she had ignored our words when I'd gone in the second time, had gone along with Henry's word until Jessica had broken rank and helped save everyone.

"Linda, Jessica, I'm sorry," I told them, then turned around and left the fire, my appetite gone.

17

I TOSSED and turned in my sleep. I'd heard whispers and rumors that some of the folks who'd been at Les's and who were now at our homestead had been part of the group that'd been kidnapped and abused. I hadn't gone seeking out the truthfulness of it, because the knowledge was painful enough knowing it had happened to somebody. Watching Linda Carpenter fall apart completely had killed any of the old anger and hate. I got it now. The puzzle pieces had been there all along. Just when I thought I had seen the big picture, another piece fell into place.

Maybe that was what life was like. You see what you want to see until confronted with the truth. How you dealt with the absolute truth shaped who you were as a human. When I'd said I was sorry to Linda, I'd truly meant it. I'd definitely meant it when I said it to Jessica, but I was sure that avenue was closed.

The night had been cooler than normal, so I put a

log in the fireplace to warm it up and make sure Grandma had some good coals so she could do her morning cooking.

"Mister Wes?" Mary's timid voice came from the hallway.

"Hey, what are you doing up?" I asked her, closing the firebox.

"I can't sleep. My mom is tossing and turning. I think she's having the bad dream again."

"You want me to see if I can mix you up some milk?" I asked her, knowing the container of powdered milk had been brought up by Emily after Grandpa had moved the coop.

"Yes please," she said, dragging a small blanket and a stuffed teddy bear behind her in the direction of the table.

I mixed the powdered milk with water, stirring, then sprinkled some cinnamon on top and sat the glass on top of the fireplace.

"Does that make it taste disgusting?" she asked, her tone turning up at the last word.

"That's how my Grandma made it for me when I couldn't sleep. Want to sit at the table?"

"Yes please."

Speaking hadn't been as much trouble for her as it had before, and the bruising had faded. In another day or two somebody was going to have to address the stitches. I'm pretty sure it was time for them to be pulled.

She got into the chair, and I saw she'd been

carrying my old blanket from when I was little. My mom had given that to me, at least that's what Grandma had said. The bear I recognized as well, but she was holding onto them so fiercely, I couldn't help but smile. I pulled a chair out and plopped her in it and pushed it in as quietly as I could.

"Where's my puppy?" I asked her.

"I think he's guarding my Momma's sleep. He's sitting right next to her on the floor."

I whistled low enough that it wasn't loud. Raider came out, slowly, stretching and yawning.

"Can I give him a treat?" Mary asked.

"I... sure," I told her, going to the fridge that had been cleaned out. It still worked like a decent cooler if it had something to act as a cold sink.

Our well water came out nice and cold. It wasn't an ideal way to keep meat cool, but Grandma was going to show the men and women how to pressure can over a fire. A tricky feat and a balancing act. I pulled one of the chunks out that Grandma had pre-diced and put in a steel bowl set over the bucket of water, and handed it to Mary.

Raider sat up and went very still next to where he'd stopped at the table.

"Here you go," Mary held it out.

Gentler than I'd ever seen him, Raider took the piece of venison from her and then went full on call of the wild. Mary giggled when he came back, nose in her hand sniffing, then cleaned it off. I was next on the list.

"Is the milk supposed to bubble?" she asked.

I turned to the stove, worried it was boiling over, and grabbed it up. The brief moments it had been up there had warmed it slightly, but nowhere got it close to boiling.

"No, it feels just perfect," I told her, handing the glass over.

She was about the most mature six-year-old I'd seen, not that I made it a point to hang out with kids beyond the occasional acquaintance who'd got married right out of high school and had kids. This one I liked, quite a bit.

"This tastes sort of funny," she said, but then went on drinking it.

"Powdered milk tastes sort of funny. Want to hear a joke?"

"Sure?" she said, hesitation in her voice, before taking another drink.

"If you eat a clown, will it taste funny?"

She sprayed milk across the table and started choking on the mouthful. I grabbed the glass before it could spill and started patting her on the back. She coughed several times, then cleared her throat. I was worried we'd been too loud and woke everyone up, but a snore from the back of the house drowned everything out. Raider? He just let out a huff and laid down at my feet.

"You're going to get me in trouble making me blow milk out of my nose!"

"And making you cough that hard," I said. "I didn't think it was *that* funny."

"It was," she said, grinning.

I got a clean dish cloth and wet it, then wiped the table down, cleaning up the mess.

"Can I have that?" she asked, pointing to the glass I'd pulled out of harm's way.

"I thought it tasted—"

She giggled and shook her head no at me. She finished the glass of milk then let out a soft burp. Raider poked his head up at that, then put it back down.

"Will you read me a book?" she asked after a long pause.

"What do you want me to read?"

"There's a book in your closet about monsters and a little boy in pajamas?"

"Where the Wild Things Are?" I asked her.

"Yes."

EMILY WAS DEFINITELY HAVING BAD DREAMS. I SNUCK IN there as quietly as I could, while she thrashed sleepily against something in the dream world. She was mumbling, but nothing coherent came out. I thought about waking her up, but even bad sleep was better than no sleep. Boy, did I know that. It took some digging, but I found the book and grabbed an old Dr. Seuss one in case she wanted another.

When I came back to the living room, Mary was on my spot on the couch, the blanket she'd brought out draped over a shoulder. She patted the spot where my pillow had been, and I sat down.

"Can I sit with you?"

She was already sitting with me.

"Sure," I said.

She scooted onto my lap and pulled the bigger blanket over. I tucked it in around us while she got comfortable and opened the book and I started to read. Raider got up and walked to the couch, jumping on the end where my feet would have gone. I tried not to grin. The log popped and the nostalgic memories of Grandma reading to me right on this very couch almost swamped me. I kept reading.

A WEIGHT SETTLED NEXT TO ME, PUSHING THE COVERS up, then settled into my side. Raider often put his nose down and curled in. I was tired, the book and the fond memories had knocked me out almost as fast as it had Mary. I didn't want to wake her, and I was comfortable. Too tired.

GRANDPA'S CHUCKLE WOKE ME UP. I RUBBED MY EYES, knowing I hadn't slept enough, but I'd slept hard. Need caffeine. Must kickstart brain. I opened my eyes to find I was sandwiched between Mary and Emily, with Raider at my feet. Emily's arms were around my chest, snoring softly on my shoulder. I looked up at Grandpa, confused.

"So you finally picked?" he asked, his voice quiet.

"I didn't pick, I just fell asleep reading the munchkin a book."

Emily stirred a bit, then started breathing the rhythm of a deep sleeper.

"Thought that one was going to kick a hole in the wall in her sleep. When she quit, I figured she must have gotten over the nightmare."

"I guess she came out here to look for Mary."

"Uh huh." Grandpa tossed me a saucy wink. "Want some coffee?"

"I'd kill for some."

He got up and filled the percolator. I watched him move; something was off this morning. He wasn't moving as good as he had been this past week. Probably sore from all the extra work. He put the percolator on the firebox, then opened it, tossing another log on there.

"Somebody fed this," he said quietly.

"I put a log on last night to make Mary some warm milk."

The little girl stirred, and Grandpa put a finger over his mouth to shush me.

"Where's Grandma?" I asked him.

"Looking for her Polaroid camera, this picture will either go in your hall of fame, or hall of shame."

I rolled my eyes and saw through the window as she walked in the yard, scattering scratch corn as she went. Grandpa was already pulling my leg. Again. There were all kinds of activity going on outside around the fire we'd used to cook. The pot was back on. They must not have eaten all the stew.

"You hungry?" Grandpa asked.

I nodded, I was always hungry. I extricated myself as best I could, Raider finally moving. Emily woke briefly, then laid back down on her side. I stretched, stiff from sleeping sitting up. At least I finally was able to sleep. Raider ran to the door, so I let him out. He took off at a run for a patch of grass and I grinned as Foghorn let the world know he was still top of the world. I thought about siccing Raider on him to get Grandma sputtering about her baby, but didn't.

I went to the bedroom, getting clothes out and headed into the bathroom to wash up. After that I felt about a million times better, and Grandma was inside.

"You sleep ok?" she asked me, looking pointedly at the couch.

"Not really. Mary woke up," I said in a hushed tone, "and I couldn't sleep anyway. I made her warm milk and cinnamon and read her a book and zonked."

"You were snoring loud enough to wake the dead," Grandpa said.

"Do you think..." Grandma looked at Emily, "Jessica and her mom..."

"I don't think we'll have any more problems with them. We sorta buried the hatchet."

"Good morning," Emily said, sitting up and stretching.

"Morning," I replied. "You sleep ok?"

"Not really," she admitted. "Had a moment where I couldn't find Mary and Raider, so I came out and found you two all curled up. I tried to carry her to bed, but she woke up. I sat down to try to wait for her to fall asleep enough again and fell asleep myself. Sorry."

"It's ok," I told her, all kinds of feelings at war with each other.

"You going to go out there and talk to them?" Grandma asked.

"After I eat maybe?"

Grandma nodded and got out her cast iron just as the percolator was finished. Grandpa took that and poured cups all around. Things might have been blasted back to the stone age, but things here hadn't changed all that much, all things considered.

A rattle of gunfire broke the morning silence, and Raider started barking. Not his warning bark, but his full on, 'I'm going to eat your face for lunch' bark. Grandpa and I leapt up. I got into his room first, grabbing the M4 and pouch of magazines I'd stored in there near his bed as he pulled out his deer rifle. We'd moved the guns in here with Mary around, but now I'd regretted that decision as it cost us time, time we might not have. A shout went up outside and Raider's bark turned into a growl.

18

THE GRASS WAS on fire in two spots. People were running while others were pumping the well handle. One of the new men went running by and pointed up the hill as a loud booming sound went off. Then screams. The grass fire was being handled, so I took off at a dead run for the sound of my dog. I didn't have far to go, at the top of the driveway a skirmish line of people was forming in cover across the street.

"Get down," Rolston screamed from behind the wooden barricade made to look like a ground blind.

I hit the deck at the edge of the road, keeping my rifle up. Raider ran to my side, pulling on my pant leg as more shots peppered the road. I scrambled onto all fours and somehow was missed as more gunshots sprayed around me. Somebody behind the barricade screamed as lead slapped into flesh. I stopped behind a large tree, pulling my dog's collar. Raider didn't want to go, he wanted to rip and shred the enemy, but where were they? I peeked around the tree as somebody opened up again. Bark flew and I ducked.

I could hear people screaming on our side of the barricade and I turned back to see Rolston mouthing to me, 'over there'.

I turned as two figures in black BDUs came into sight about where we'd buried the three men on four wheelers we'd killed at the start of summer. I lined them up in my sights as Grandpa's rifle went off. The figure on the right was blown off his feet, Grandpa's shot having gone all way through. The spray of blood was impressive. Where had Grandpa come from? My vision started to tunnel out as I pulled the trigger. The bullet caught the man in the back as he was looking at the downed man in surprise. It tumbled him off his feet and I chanced looking down the road again.

The bushes were alive, but with friend or foe? Everybody knew the Black BDUs meant Henry and Lance's people.

"Cease fire," somebody from down the road yelled through a bullhorn.

I looked back and saw rifles bristling from fortified positions, and somebody rolling on the ground.

"I've got a message," the bullhorn blasted again.

"What?" I screamed back, my voice cracking.

"Send us the Marshall kid and the Flagg kid and we'll let you live."

Marshall. I hadn't seen him lately, he'd been staying in the barn with the rest.

"Look around you," the voice boomed, "your entire property is surrounded."

The figure I'd shot got up but made no move to raise his gun. His free hand was rubbing something, and I realized that he'd been wearing a slim vest of some sort. I'd taken it to be a tactical vest like the man Grandpa had shot, but he must have been wearing a plate carrier. Grandpa's bullet had gone clean through the other guy, who'd quit moaning and twitching. The movement around us seemed to stop and figures in black and camo BDUs with vests stood up. I would have liked to have said it looked like a ton of people, but it wasn't. They were outside the fougasse cannons. Otherwise, in range. Heh. I looked back at Rolston and made a circle with my hands.

"Boom?" I asked him spreading my hands outwards.

He grinned and spoke into a radio. The earth shook and everyone hit the dirt.

"HOW MANY?" GRANDMA ASKED, USING A SHOVEL TO point.

"Fourteen, ma'am," Sherriff ...Jackson said.

"Ours?" I asked him.

"Two. One poked his head up when he shouldn't, and the other got splinters in his arm from a lucky shot that missed his torso. He'll make it."

I didn't need to be told what happened to the one

who poked his head up. His body was laying apart from the dead that Henry's group had sent.

"I'm sorry," I told him. "Somebody you were close with?"

Rolston and Sherriff shrugged. Somebody they knew, not a deputy, but a survivor. Les would know them. I hadn't seen him or the Carpenters all morning.

"Good loot?" I asked them.

"Lots of stuff to scavenge, but some of it... Those chains did a wicked number to the men in the truck."

"I saw," I said softly.

The chain had come out of the cannon, taking off the top of the cab of a pickup as it came apart, tearing everything and everyone behind it into bloody chunks. It was gruesome.

"Well, that'll teach them, won't it," Grandma said, then spat on the ground.

"I'm worried that it'll only inflame them more," Rolston said softly. "Linda and Jessica have been asking for you," he told me.

"I'll go talk to them in a moment. Have you guys checked the bodies for radios and frequencies? Scrambler codes?"

"Yes, and we hit pay dirt. They'd been changing things up since your family busted out of there. We're back on their network again."

"Good," I said softly. "I need one of those radios."

"There's only so many, and the men—"

"Uncle Will, don't..."

Sheriff Jackson lifted a foot then lowered it as if

he'd stepped in something, then walked over to a pile of equipment and tossed me a radio. I caught it, getting smears of congealed blood on me and my shirt. Ruined, I used my shirt to finish wiping it off the best I could. Clipping it to my belt, I pulled my shirt off and wiped down my hands.

"How did they get in so close with the vehicles?" I asked them.

"Muffled, custom job. Most of them probably walked in from somewhere. Most of them escaped on foot. They really brought a lot of men to take you and that Marshall kid back. Enough to have done the job."

"Looks like your defenses worked out well, huh?"

Somebody behind me mumbled something about force multipliers. Sheriff turned and started talking to the group of defenders who'd been prepared, ignoring me. He'd lost a man, had another wounded. As much as I was involved here, I really wasn't involved in the defensive plans the way the group that came from Les's place was. I hadn't been pulling patrol or guard duty. I'd offered, but had been told a polite no, that they had things handled.

"Let's go see if all this ruckus has caused my hens to quit laying," Grandma huffed.

"Go on ahead," I told her, "I'm going to find Jessica and Linda."

Raider had lost interest in the fight soon after it was done and was sunning himself in the lawn near the scorched marks where the grass had burned. The man Grandpa had shot had tossed a grenade downhill, thinking we'd been in the tall grass hiding. All he'd done was give away his position and burned some grass. Grandpa said he was silhouetted against the sky, and the shot had been easy. Then Grandpa had gone back inside, slamming the door. I would have to check on him later, I knew a little bit about why he was avoiding people right now.

It was a weird day and I was thankful, because it could have gone worse. I headed into the barn with my pup at my side, the carbine over my shoulder in that one-point drop sling. Marshall was waiting by the big door, letting the sunlight hit his face.

"How you doing?" I asked him.

"I'm... he's not still mad at me, is he?" Marshall pointed at my dog.

"No, he knows you belong here now. You doing ok? Getting enough to eat? People being nice to you?" The last bit worried me, as he'd been at the Crater, apparently at the same time as some of the people in the barn.

"Oh yeah, they've been nice to me. I've been working with some of the littler kids, trying to teach them how to read and stuff. They seem to like that."

I smiled. He liked being around kids, because even though he was an adult, he was still a kid at heart, locked into a never changing innocence.

"Jessica and Linda in here?" I asked, even though I knew they were, I could see them.

"Oh yeah, with the ladies," he said pointing.

"Thanks buddy," I said, patting him on the side of the arm.

The ladies had formed somewhat of a small group sitting on the bottom bunks of two rows of beds. They were chatting and consoling one woman who had just lost her husband. Jessica saw me walking toward them and stood up, waving. I saw the cuffs were off her and her mother. Both had changed clothing, probably while theirs was being washed. Had to have borrowed it from some of the other ladies unless they had clothing in their pack.

Jessica was wearing a plaid button up shirt, the sleeves rolled up. Linda was in an old faded T-shirt that sported Oscar the Grouch. Both had on jeans, but were barefoot.

"Is she going to be OK?" I asked as I got near them.

Jessica wrapped her arms around me, pulling me in close, and started crying on my shoulder. I dropped the bloody shirt to the floor as Linda got up and hugged her from behind, her nails raking my arms lightly as she tried to make contact with me. I was sort of shocked at this reaction, but I hugged both back. Raider chuffed, giving his approval over something I had no idea what he was talking about. After a few moments, Jessica let go, forcing her mom back.

I was choked up seeing this, and pointed to an empty area, next to the stall where we'd made love on a blanket covered straw bale. They followed and I opened the padlock from my keys, allowing both to walk in. Linda sat down in Grandpa's chair and I motioned Jessica to my spot. She shook her head, her arms wrapped around herself. I sat in the chair instead and let her work out whatever she had going on for what felt like minutes.

"That's the widow?" I asked, pointing over my shoulder.

"Yes," Linda answered. "Friends of friends of Les."

"Sorry," I said, not sure why I was apologizing for somebody none of us really knew.

"I thought you'd died," Jessica said, choked up, then started breathing again, her breaths coming out in gasps.

"Why?" I asked her.

"We were still cuffed, and they wouldn't let us leave the barn, and when I saw you go across the street you fell and—"

"Somebody yelled duck, and I didn't hesitate to stop drop and roll," I told her. "Only a scratch from where somebody took a potshot at a tree and got me with splinters," I pointed at my face.

"They want you and Marshall back. Bad," Linda said dryly.

"Apparently, though I can't figure out why."

"Marshall to get Lance's boys under control again, and you to make drugs for them."

"We don't even have the chemicals and—"

"Methamphetamine is pretty easy to make, especially with all the pharmacies raided," Linda said quietly.

"I'm no Walter White," I said. "If they know what to get, they probably know how to make it anyways."

"Could be another reason they want you," Jessica said quietly, wiping the tears away.

"What's that?" I asked as Raider crawled up on the straw bale and laid down.

"Every time you're around, things blow up and their people die."

Revenge. Was it that simple? I'd taken away their harem and trade goods when I'd started the explosions that led to Jessica rescuing the girls. I'd broken our group out of Linda's bunker and set the trap that killed more of their men, and now they'd come here, and we'd lit a couple cannons against them, a defense they'd missed until it was too late.

"Either or. You're a marked man. Both sides want you," Linda said.

"I bet you'd like to let them have me, wouldn't you?" I was being unfair, but I found there was a small ember of anger in my gut I thought had been put out.

"I... I'm sorry Wes. Oh hell, for a lot of things. If you only understood—"

"I do, and it's ok. It's over now. I finally figured things out. Listen though, we picked up one of Henry's radios," I showed her.

"They'll change frequencies soon," Jess said, wiping her eyes again and holding her hand out for the radio.

I gave it to her, and she finally sat down in the shine

stall, pushing Raider aside a bit. I looked out the stall door, seeing we had a little bit of an audience, including the tear streaked widow who strode in, looking for a place to sit.

"Raider, let the lady sit," I told him.

Raider grumbled and got down, then decided to jump on my lap, hitting me in a bad spot before turning and settling down, hanging off both ends of the chair. I tried not to puke.

"Wes, this is Carla," Jessica said softly, indicating a woman who'd walked up to the doorway, her face streaked from crying. She was Linda's age or there-abouts. Brown hair, jeans that hung loose but belted tight, wearing a cotton flannel button up.

"I'm so sorry Carla," I said, not knowing what to say.

"I want to hear what they have to say. That we killed their men. That we'll be killing more of them."

She was fired up now and had the same look of sadness and rage I'd only seen in Emily. Jessica looked to me and I shrugged. This would be all over the homestead soon anyways. Jessica and Linda nodded and turned the radio on. We listened as different teams reported in, a familiar voice taking reports until I heard someone call him Spider. The leader who'd taken over Lance's crew and was tied into Henry. How much this Spider's gig and how much of it was Henry's?

According to the reports we listened to, more than 25 people hadn't reported in, of the seventy or so they said they sent out. They might be talking in code, but we knew we'd killed 14. And 70 people? That'd be everyone they had or almost close to it. Wasn't it? I shivered as we listened to some of the men rage about the losses they'd taken, and how the intel was shit.

Intel, they had intel on us. How? Probably the same way we had done it with Jessica's group before they had gone rogue. They were watching from afar, beyond our defenses. They probably hadn't zeroed in on us the first couple of days when we'd moved the big defenses into place, but later when we were scouring the area for supplies and moving furniture to the barn.

The scattered reports came in, a few more men had walked to a checkpoint, bloodied, wounded and unable to radio in for some reason. That left a few more unaccounted for that we knew of.

"Why do they want you and the kid?" Carla asked quietly as the radio started beeping from a dead battery.

Jessica turned it off, but I was rocking slightly, Raider awake for once on my lap.

"My guess for Marshall, it's to get Lance's boys under control again. For Wes though, it could be anything. Probably revenge." Linda was matter of fact. "Or the fact he's the only one around here who's a chemistry major."

"Chemistry?" Carla asked, me, her eyes red and puffy.

"When they were keeping me, I was able to make them some stuff. Chloroform, stuff like that. Seemed really interested when I mentioned I could make other things in theory, if I had the materials."

"Drugs?" she asked.

"Drugs, explosives, probably chemical weapons if they had thought of it."

"Chemical weapons?" Linda said, an eyebrow going up.

"Probably not, but I know how to make some crude stuff out of household items like I was doing—"

"Wes," Jessica said, her hand going to her mouth.

"I had the supplies needed to break us out of the bunker in my backpack when Henry made his move. Wouldn't have been lethal unless the people were exposed for more than a few minutes, breathing in the gas."

"Please promise me, no gas," Jessica asked.

"What?" I was surprised.

"Please, I've seen what gas has done, what it can do."

Ok, no gas. I just nodded to her in agreement.

"Do we have a preacher here?" Carla asked.

"I don't know," I murmured softly.

Raider got down and headed out of the stall, something having attracted his attention.

"Jessica, where's your dogs?" I asked.

She hesitated, then when Linda nodded to her, she turned to me. "The Gutheries got out when the firing first started. They talked to me when I was burying..." her words trailed off and she went silent a moment before picking up again. "That's when I knew something was wrong. They walked out to talk amongst themselves and when the firing started, they bugged out. We've got a small fall back spot a couple miles away from the bunker. We met them there after we left here."

"Are they monitoring the radios?" I asked.

"Yes, they're the ones who told me where my mom was when..." these silences were becoming uncomfortable. *When I'd shot her mom.*

"Have you learned anything about Spider's group, the PMCs?" I asked Linda, getting up to stretch.

"Yes," Linda said, pausing to organize her thoughts. "Dirtbags, all of them former military, most of them dishonorable discharges or stone-cold mercenaries with no scruples. No love for the oath. Mostly did large scale private security. Other than that, you probably know as much as we do. Killion Group Reserve. KGR, call themselves Keggers."

"Where were they headquartered?" I asked.

"We think it's somewhere on the West Coast, but they were doing a large training down here when they all got stranded. Lots of equipment, not much on vehicles on site. Not sure about how much ammo or explosives."

"Explosives are everywhere," I murmured.

"No artillery, no mortars," Jessica piped up. "They said they'd love to use it on us if they had it when we first broke out."

"And Spider's in charge of the PMCs?" I asked.

Both ladies nodded as Carla excused herself, and went outside, probably to say her last goodbyes to her husband.

"What do we know about him?" I asked.

"Larry Killion, aka Spider. Loves to ride Harleys. His inner circle is almost cult-like in their loyalty and devotion. Probably why they were snagging..." Linda looked out at the group in the barn and lowered her voice, "why they were taking women. To keep their men in check."

"The night I... got shot and a cracked skull," I paused, rubbing the new scar tissue on my forehead, "I overheard two of them talking about trading them for supplies."

"Wouldn't surprise me," Linda said. "In third world countries, the slave and human trafficking trade is very real. Probably saw a similar situation here and saw what they had and were trying to trade for what they needed."

"That's disgusting," I said softly.

"It didn't really hit home until last night," Linda said. "Dave and I were so scared of what Henry was threatening to do, we just followed along even if in my heart I knew it was wrong."

"Water under the bridge," I said softly. "Do you want to get the Gutheries and your dogs here?"

"Yes, and we need to make plans on getting better intel and find out what's happening next," Linda said, "that is... if you'll have us?"

Jessica stood up and pulled me in close and kissed the daylights out of me. I wrapped my hands around her waist, hugging onto her fiercely until somebody coughed politely in the doorway. I broke the kiss to turn and see Emily standing there. I was expecting anger, rage, insane jealousy. Instead, she was smiling like she'd won the lottery.

"Grandma said if you don't eat your breakfast, she's gonna give it to the dog, and Mary said she's going to drink all your cinnamon milk if you don't hurry."

"I—"

"Go eat," Linda said, "It's been a long day."

"Come with me?" I asked the ladies.

Emily's smile grew. I walked out and waited to see if the ladies would follow. They did, but Emily pulled Jessica aside and whispered something to her. Jessica whispered back, then noticed my puzzled look, giggled, whispered some more, and then both were walking my way.

"What was that?" I asked Linda.

"Wouldn't you like to know," she laughed, and they left me standing there confused about what had just happened.

Jessica and Linda made radio contact with Margie and Curt, and they agreed to meet us halfway in a few days' time. They didn't want to travel so soon after we'd kicked the hornet's nest. That made sense to me, but Linda made a sour face. I'd gone out hunting again and set out several sets of snares for small game, and one deer snare near the area where Linda had taken her potshot at me at the Crater. That was how I found myself wandering with Jessica, both of us decked out in camouflage for the third morning in a row, Raider at my side.

"You worried leaving his scent around will scare off game?" Jessica asked.

"Not this time. I think all the shenanigans the other day scared game into hunkering down. I dunno."

"Where did your deer snare go?" she asked as we came to the spot on the trail where I'd set it.

"Oh goodie," I said, rubbing my hands together and kneeling.

The bark was rubbed off in one spot as something had scraped by a tree. I pointed that out and had Raider come to smell it.

"Go fetch," I told him.

Raider let out a bark and went on ahead of us.

"You worried he'll scare it off or...?"

"Naw, if we got it, it's down," I told her as Raider started barking.

We hadn't trained him to track, but telling him to fetch seemed to trigger an instinct. We found him a couple dozen steps later. He quit barking and sat, his tongue hanging out of his mouth in a doggy smile.

"Good job, buddy," I told him. "Back up and let me make sure it's dead."

"What if it's not?" Jessica asked.

"Kick a hole in yer belly," I said, only half joking.

She took a step back and called Raider to heel at her side. Of course, the dog listened to her, when he'd hardly do it for me. I pulled my belt knife off and hacked a long, straight, skinny limb off some brush nearby and hacked the smaller offshoots until I had a good five-foot-long straight-ish stick. I poked the deer in the eyeball. When it didn't move, I tossed the stick. It was another doe, this one a little smaller than the one I'd shot the last time.

The camlock had done its job, so had the log I'd used as a drag. I released it, then rolled up the gnarled wire, stuffing it into a cargo pocket.

"Going to clean it here?" Jessica asked.

"You ever see this done?" I asked her.

"Just once, but not enough to do it myself."

I grinned.

"Oh, hell no," she said, backing up.

"What's the matter?" I asked, standing up and offering her my belt knife.

"Not until I've seen it done a couple of times."

"That's so girly," I teased.

"That's because despite being an American Badass, capital letters, I am in fact. A. Girl."

Nodding to her, I pulled my pack off and got out some cordage and tied the legs of the deer together, then handed her my pack and gun. She watched as I hoisted the deer up and over, finding a good spot to center the load and not throw off my balance. She kinda opened and closed her mouth, but in the end didn't say anything.

"Raider, want to go home and get some good treats?" I asked him.

He barked happily and ran to my side, bumping my hip with his noggin, almost spilling me and the deer down.

"I guess that means yes," Jessica told me. "Same way out as in?"

"You got it."

I MADE A POINT OF SHOWING ANYBODY WHO WAS

interested how to clean the deer, telling them that this one hadn't been bled out like I'd normally do with a fresh kill, so it might taste different than the one I'd shot the day Linda had been hunting me. They'd nodded, and several turned green, but the small group of kids watched, fascinated. Mary was the only one who insisted on helping, as I hung the deer to skin it. It was easier than doing it on the ground, because I could pull the skin quicker than I could skin it with a knife.

This time around, everything was kept from the deer. Nothing was going to waste according to Grandma. The heart was cooked over the fire that seemed to be constantly going now and then cut into small pieces and shared around. It was Grandpa's idea, so I didn't mind. When we started throwing bones in Grandma's big pot, Grandpa came to me, a shit-eating grin on his face.

"Want to add even more variety?" he asked, his old satchel over his shoulders, the one he carried small game hunting.

"Sure?" I asked, curious.

He undid the leather ties and pulled the flap open. I started laughing softly. He'd gotten two rabbits and a quail.

"How? You set some snares out?" I asked, still cutting meat.

"Rabbit boxes," he said with a grin. "Right behind the new privies."

"Probably tastes like dookie then," Grandma said, without looking up.

I couldn't help it, I started laughing, so did the kids who were watching everything.

"Yeah, go ahead. We going to can any of this?" I asked Grandma, pointing at the meat that had been put on the skin side of the deer hide.

"Depends," she said softly, "I don't think we need it as much as these folks do."

Ah, true. If we canned it, people would assume we were keeping it. Food was still a hot button issue with some folks.

"Want me to do the honors?" I asked Grandpa, noting the necks of all the critters had been expertly broken.

"You're already bloody, why not." He dumped them on the ground near the hide and walked away whistling.

"Did you get my daughter all disgusting?" Emily asked, walking up with Mary, the little girl caught red-handed, literally.

"She insisted on helping, you didn't watch?" I asked.

Emily looked pale green and shook her head violently.

"Cleans up easy peasy. Miss Mary, want to see if somebody would run the hand pump for you?" I asked, thinking the ladies hadn't come here to just pick on me for Mary's dirty hand.

"Yes, Mister Wes," she said, laughing, and headed to the pump where a boy near her age was pumping water into a bucket.

One of these days I needed to sit down and get names for everyone and try to remember them. Flash cards. It was hard, because it seemed like we'd had some new folks come in at some point.

"What's on your minds, ladies?" I asked, noticing the two of them sharing looks.

"We've got some intel," Emily said, as if she used words like this all the time.

"Really?" I asked, putting the knife down, but Jessica shooed me back to work with a motion.

"I'm almost done here anyway," I said, then remembered the smaller game and started processing that.

Emily turned a tad greener and let out a small urking sound, and put her hand up as if she had burped. I hurried.

"Henry and Spider split their forces up. We found out where they moved the RVs and campers. They're still working together, but there seems to be more of a purpose-driven agenda now."

"What's that?" I asked them.

"They're collecting people again."

The words made me shudder.

"Women and children?" I asked, already knowing the answer.

"And men too," Emily said, glancing my way for a moment. "Finding people who hid from the government forces and offering them food if they'll join up."

"What do they do to the men who *won't* join up?" I asked her.

"It's not ... good. Make them slaves if they are lucky.

They're trying to get a couple of the abandoned farm fields harvested right now. Some of the equipment works, but most of the labor comes from humans."

"At least they're wearing clothing that makes it easy to point out the bad guys," I said, distractedly.

"It gets worse," Emily said, looking at Jessica.

"Some of the men and women they are talking about joining up with them willingly, to help them kidnap and attack others," Jessica said, and I couldn't help but look at the ground and take a deep breath before my anger got ahead of me.

"So no easy way to identify good from bad any more. Got any worse news?"

"They've gotten several armored trucks now. Not like the banks used to transport money, but like MRAPS, armored Hummers. Some have heavy machine guns mounted on the top turrets. We're not sure, but I think they either raided a local Reserve armory, or they had people join up. I think what we saw was more twenty-year-old surplus bought on the black market, but I'm not one hundred percent for sure," Jessica said. We were drawing a small crowd, but they were giving us space.

"How'd you find out?" I asked Jessica.

"Mom cracked their encryption codes and now knows what frequencies to monitor. We're setting up a communications spot if we can find a place..."

I nodded. "Would it help if we had a huge antenna?"

"Wait, what? You've got one?"

"Yeah, you've been sleeping under it. Grandpa had an idea to have a pirate radio station but—"

"Mom!" Jessica took off, running like a shot. Raider barked happily and gave chase instead of drooling over what I was doing.

"So," Emily said, kicking the ground.

"So ... how did you and Jessica finally become friends?"

"What are you talking about?" she asked, looking at me from side eye so she didn't have to see me pulling the skin off the quail, taking the feathers with it.

"That night in the barn she kissed me, you said something to her ... wait, before that, you looked like the cat that ate the canary!"

She looked at me and laughed. Mary looked up from where she had been bossing the boy to pump harder and waved a hand that was running pink rivulets off her arm. I waved back with the knife.

"What?"

"You guys can be dense sometimes," she said with a grin.

"We really can, so how about you, I dunno, fill me in?"

"How about we not and say we did?"

I was going to keep poking but decided to let it go. She'd tell me in her own way, in her own time.

"Wes," Linda's voice called from the barn.

"Yeah?" I called back, not getting up from the literal bloody mess I was dealing with, as I started on a rabbit.

"Do you have any wire to go with this antenna?" Her words echoed.

"Ask my Grandpa," I called back.

The barn had become a hive of activity and cursing. Several ladders were dragged out of storage, and by the time I'd finished with the last rabbit and had all the boned pieces of it in the stew pot, four sections of the antenna were laid out in the driveway.

"Where are they going to put that?" Rolston asked, walking up.

"No clue. I'm not a radio guy. You are, though; how about you mansplain to the Carpenter ladies how it works."

"Hell no," he said. "You know, isn't it funny how everyone forgave those two so fast?"

"I ... I sort of thought so, but I guess it made sense. When Linda started crying and apologized, something in me..." I squeezed my fist together, making red droplets hit the ground.

"Yeah, that, and how your other girlfriend pulled a gun on her. Holy shit, man. I thought she was going to ice Linda right there."

"Emily isn't my other girlfriend," I told him, grinning.

"She sure cares the world about you," he said. "If she isn't your woman, aren't you worried with Jessica back in your life?"

"Jessica and I weren't really, I mean it wasn't... Nothing like... Oh hell. It's one huge complicated thing, man."

"I know, and every single lady is either wanting to kill you, scratch your eyes out, or protect you between the three of them."

"Wait, I know who wanted to kill me, but which one wanted to scratch my eyes out?"

"It changes day by day," he said with a grin, then tipped his hat and walked off.

I cursed. Nobody would tell me anything. Emily suddenly becoming genuinely happy with me and Jessica back to where we were a couple weeks back was a little unsettling. But it wasn't faked or forced unless she was the universe's best actress ever, and that girl wore her emotions for all to see.

20

DURING THE NEXT TWO WEEKS, Linda and a crew of the residents installed the antenna tower next to the road, up the hill. Instead of pouring a pad, they put it up against the old power pole, securing it to that every couple feet. Using the dead power lines, phone lines, and miscellaneous bibs and bobs (Grandpa's phrase), they got enough wire to run it to the barn. Jessica and Linda had already figured out I had power and a way to charge batteries in the barn, so increasing that was the next thing on the agenda.

"WE NEED MORE POWER TO REALLY RUN THE communications equipment we've got and charge the batteries for the handhelds," Linda told me. We were in the stall where I kept my charge controller and batteries that I used for the water pump.

"We can always add more solar and batteries. See what works, what doesn't?" I added hopefully.

Grandpa walked in and leaned in the doorway, holding Mary on his hip. She waved shyly at me, and I waved back. That little girl was growing on me in a big way. She craved male attention and had latched onto Grandpa and I in a way she hadn't with anybody else. Grandma loved her to pieces, but Mary was still a momma's girl in that regard.

"What about those towable road construction signs with the solar panels?" he asked, putting Mary down.

"The ones with the blinking warnings on the signs—"

"Or the ones that tell you how fast you're going?" Jessica asked, sneaking up on us.

"That would work," I told them, "as long as nobody has scavenged them already."

Jessica grinned. "Well I'm pretty sure there's a bunch they didn't. At least four or five."

She explained where they were, and thankfully, it was in the opposite direction that Spider and the Keggers had been operating out of.

"How do we do this?" I asked her.

"We send out a few trucks at a time, with two or three people working ahead of them as a sort of scouting team. Once things are clear, we can call in the convoy to come tow the trailers back. We can get most of them in one trip that way."

"What about hitting a road construction company's

old warehouse?" I asked them. "They probably have those things stored all over the place, right?"

"Not always," Jessica said, "Dad worked for one when I was a kid. A lot of their equipment is stored right at the jobsite. When they finish one job, they take it to the next and so on until it has to be fixed or replaced."

"But they'd have spare parts?" I asked, a hopeful tone in my voice.

"What are you looking to power up besides the communication gear?" Grandpa asked, curious.

"How about more lights here for instance, maybe get some semblance of normalcy back?"

"Your grandma would love to have a working refrigerator again," he said, rubbing his chin. "How many panels you think we can fit up on this barn's roof?"

"We fill the entire roof, we can power the barn, the house, and a lot more," I said, grinning.

"I like this idea," Grandpa said.

"And what are you talking about we?" I asked Jessica, poking her in the side, making her jump and slap my hand away.

"I thought you, me, and my mom should go ahead and scout—"

"I need to be here for the defenses and radio equipment," Linda interrupted.

"I'd go," Grandpa said, rubbing his stomach. "But I haven't been feeling right lately. Damn arthritis."

"Why don't you let my mommy go with you then?" Mary asked, making everyone turn and look at the little girl. "Nobody but Grandma Flagg will let her help with anything, and I think she's really, really bored. Plus, she likes you, Mister Wes."

We all had a chuckle at that, and I walked over, kneeling and giving her a hug. I fought back my emotions as the little girl put her arms around my neck and tried to crush me back.

"I think he knows how much your mom cares for him," Grandpa told her as I was released from the clutches of nearly losing my man card.

"Oh yeah, lots and lots. And now for some reason, she's Miss Jessica's friend too, but they don't hang out enough, so you should take my mom. And maybe that yucky Chris."

"The little boy?" I asked her, surprised.

"Yeah, the other girls said he's got cooties. When you gave me your blood, I thought I was immune to cooties, but he keeps picking these little yellow flowers for me. Yuck!"

We all had a grin at that, and I told her to go get her mom so we could talk. She took off in a hurry, running the entire way, Raider taking up the chase from just outside the barn and making her laugh at concert volume.

"Makes things almost seem normal, doesn't it?" Linda asked, a rare smile tugging at the side of her mouth.

"I don't know. I was the little screaming kid growing up here. Grandpa would know better," I said, pointing to him.

"I miss those days. Your mom was a lot..." He turned abruptly and walked off, his gait unsteady.

I knew he hadn't been drinking as much lately; we were running low on shine, something I planned on fixing soon.

"Is he ok?" Linda asked quietly.

"I don't know. My mom gave me up when I was little. I don't really remember her," I admitted. "Grandma used to write to her but..."

"Wes, I'm sorry," Jessica said, pulling me in tight for a hug.

"Thanks," I told her, kissing her gently. "But I really don't remember her. I remember Grandpa and Grandma. I remember throwing chicken scratch and a long procession of mean roosters. When one got too old, Grandma would grow out a younger rooster and leave him alone. We usually processed the younger roos though," I said with a grin, reliving memories of being chased by a long procession of birds who resembled Foghorn.

"Here comes Emily," Jessica said softly, still in my arms.

"You want her to come with us?" I asked, leaning in and kissing her hard, making her breath catch.

"Come on you two," Linda said, slapping my shoulder.

I broke the kiss and backed up just as Emily walked through the barn and headed our way.

"Mary said you guys ... am I interrupting something?" she asked as Linda edged her way out the doorway.

"No," I said, letting Jess go. "We've got a plan to restore power to most of the farm. It's not going to be as difficult as I thought, but we need a team to go ahead and scout things out."

"And you want me to be with the scouts?" she asked, an eyebrow raised.

"You're smart, you're calm under fire and, honestly, we'd just be making sure things ahead are safe for trucks and more people to come through. Most of the military and law enforcement people are probably needed here as they've got more experience in defending the place."

"You said 'we'. The three of us?" Her eyebrow arched further.

"Yeah," Jessica said. "Unless you don't want—"

"Oh no, I'm glad. I just wasn't sure. I'd love to get out of the house some. I love it here, don't get me wrong, but people kind of avoid me for some reason."

"Probably because you pulled a Dirty Harry killer pistol out on me," Jessica said, grinning.

"That scared them? I was just trying to make a point! I really wouldn't have."

"Now we get to the good stuff. You can keep filling me in on things," I said, rubbing my hands together.

Jessica and Emily shared a look then chuckled, shaking their heads.

"What?" I asked.

"Oh, Wes," Jessica said, "There's a time and a place

for that kind of information." She dropped a wink and pulled on the bottom of my shirt.

I could feel the flush hit as my skin turned red. Emily laughed, pointing. This time it was me shaking my head.

"When do we go, and how far ahead of the trucks should we be?"

"Let's go first thing in the morning. If possible, we'll take the quads," Jessica said, nodding to the three we'd liberated from the guys chasing Les.

I winced, knowing Emily would recognize at least one of them.

She looked back where they were mostly under a tarp. "I know how to ride the green one."

And that was that.

21

LINDA AND JESSICA briefed the teams they put together. I hated to do it, but I handed my keys over to somebody Deputy Rolston had vouched for. I had a hitch on my truck but wasn't sure it was heavy duty enough to tow one of those. In case it wasn't, I packed a small tool case in a canvas bag I strapped to the front luggage rack of the blue Honda Four-Trax I was going to be riding. We topped off the gas tanks. Emily's quad would be carrying two five gallon jugs mixed with our dwindling stocks of gasoline and moonshine. Since she was the smallest and lightest of all three, it made more sense to me.

Until she got out her lever action and the BFR. The revolver was hanging off her shoulder diagonally in a bandoleer that looked custom made. I wasn't going to argue with this one, so when she put one of the big cans of fuel on my rear luggage rack, I just did the manly thing. I nodded without comment, latched it down, and followed her lead as we rode out.

None of us were wearing helmets, but we had people stationed to the northwest of the farm in the direction we were going, and they reported no movement of the Keggers. Jessica and Emily roared out of the driveway, leaving me choking on dust.

"You stay here and watch over the family," I told Raider.

He sat next to me as I fired up the quad. Up the road I could see them coming to a stop, the four wheelers idling as they talked side by side. Girls. Someday somebody better clue me in, because I was starting to develop a complex.

"Good boy, stay," I told him, then fired mine up and drove up the driveway, the four-wheel drive quad making easy work of the grade.

The ladies quit talking as I approached, and Jessica threw a follow me gesture, and they both took off again. I hit the throttle and caught up with them after a few minutes of bumpy riding, my rifle banging into my kidneys. The trucks would be a little ways behind us, giving us a twenty minute head start. I'd given Mary a hug before I'd left the house, and she'd told me I better keep her mom safe. I'd promised, and that was that. Grandma had cooked, but then had gone into the bedroom with Grandpa who was sleeping in.

The sky was overcast, threatening rain. I wore my usual of jeans and a flannel, but I could feel the temperature dropping even with the wind in my face from driving the quads. I was both nervous and loving the feeling of freedom. Nervous, because we'd have to slow down soon and take our time and pray that our last lookouts this way hadn't been snuck up on. It felt like almost as soon as we had left, we were slowing down, rolling to a stop.

Jessica got off her quad, approaching a wooden barricade across the road, manned by our people. It was the furthest spot we were watching, and the barricade was mostly to slow access and give the scouts an opportunity to see who was coming and going. The only ones who had to worry were Lance, Henry, and the KGR men with those associated with them.

"Hey, guys," Jessica said, turning her quad off.

"Miss Carpenter, no news to report, but we're the last set of eyes."

"Thank you, Max," she told the middle-aged man. "We'll radio the convoy in about ten minutes and get them on the road."

"Ok, they know how long to wait in between stops?"

Jessica explained that this would give us time and space, in case we were ambushed and attacked: for them to either help us defend, or so the entire group didn't get wiped out at once. With us being out front, we were in bigger danger, but Jessica had pointed out something when she'd talked to Emily. Emily had been with us when we were last attacked. She'd done her share of shooting under pressure, and she had killed. The last part made me uncomfortable, but I think her savage side had always been there. It had been freed up as she celebrated and mourned the loss of her husband, who'd terrorized her for years.

"They're all set, plus we're on the same frequencies," Jessica said, pointing to her radio then her earbud. "Give a girl a ring if you see anything I need to know about."

"If I give you a ring, your boyfriend might toss me outta the joint," he teased back.

I fought off reacting at the creeping red going up Jessica's neck and ears and gave him a quick wave.

"We'll be in touch," I told him as Jessica fired up her quad and started rolling slow.

I followed the two ladies. Our plan was to ride slow for ten minutes, watching everything, wait ten minutes and use the silence to see if we were being followed. We'd use our binoculars as we could, then keep on going. I was mostly going along for the ride here, except I was the one who knew about the solar setup, and ... heck, that was why Jessica wanted me to go, and to torture me with her and Emily talking and not sharing. They were talking about me if I had to guess, because they'd look right at me then laugh and claim innocence. I drove slowly, barely keeping up so we weren't all driving in a line. Emily dropped back and drove next to me.

"Everything ok?" she called.

"Yeah, why?" I asked her.

"You're being a sourpuss lately."

"I am not," I called back, swerving to miss a large

branch that had blown down and was left in the middle of the road.

"You're now in the middle of a small community that you've helped build and feed, and you've gone silent lately. You hang out with Mary, but you brood—"

"First sign in sight," Jessica called back, a touch of annoyance in her voice.

"Sorry, I'll try not to be such a sourpuss," I told Emily and then goosed the throttle, shooting forward.

"Somebody's tried to scavenge this," Jessica said.

One of the solar panels was loose, one was missing, and one of the batteries were gone. The charge controller was still there. Unless we wanted to hook everything up, there wasn't any way to see if what we had was any good.

"Want me to strip it and let one of the trucks take the components when they get here?" I asked her.

"How long to disconnect everything?" Jess asked.

"Ten to fifteen minutes max?"

Yeah," Jessica said, "go ahead. Emily, will you stay and watch his back? I'm going to roll slow ahead and split the difference so we don't lose time."

"You can count on me," she said. "You sure you're ok going solo?"

"Sorta trained for this kind of thing," Jessica told her with a grin.

"Let me get started," I told her and gave her a quick wave.

She waved back, telling us to watch ourselves and then rode off. We'd made better time than I thought, and I didn't remember this sign being here. A lot had happened though, and this route took us away from town, a direction I hadn't gone through since I'd been in Little Rock. I shrugged it off and opened my toolkit, getting out an adjustable wrench and a small socket set that usually rode in my truck.

"Do you think life will ever get back to normal?" Emily asked as I worked on the set of bolts holding the solar panels down.

"I hope so. I think we were hit with a solar storm. I don't really know if anybody knows why some things work and some don't, but if there's enough stuff left working to restore power and utilities, it shouldn't take too long. I hope."

"I hope you're right," Emily said from right behind me.

I was working on getting one of the bolts out when she put her arms around me, pressing her body in close against my back. Her nails scratched my chest, her breath hot on my neck.

"Everything is different now," she said.

My body broke out into goose bumps, and I dropped my tools.

"No, just hold still," she said, her hands moving up and down my chest, around my shoulders. "You're in love with Jessica. This is my only chance... I want you to know that part of me will always love you. I won't mess that up for you. But I want to imagine if things were different..." her words trailed off, and she moved away from me. I turned, and she gave me a quick kiss on the cheek, then backed off.

"Emily," I said, wanting to explain.

"No, sorry. I perved you, but no harm no foul. I didn't mean to fall asleep with you that other night, and I'm really happy for you and Jessica. Maybe a little jealous from time to time, but I ... shit, I think part of me clings to you and the idea of what life might be like between you and me because you've done so much for us. You're such a good influence for Mary, and she adores you. If life were different and you weren't already in love with someone ... a girl has to dream sometime. Or until she finds herself with her own version of Jason Momoa."

I grinned, rubbing my hands over my arms. "I do love her," I said, not knowing what else to say.

"Then you should tell her. Life is too short. Love is important; it's worth nurturing and holding close to your heart."

"You've been reading my grandma's magazines again?" I asked, never hearing her talk like this.

"No, just her naughtier Harlequin books." She gave me a wicked grin. "Now, what can I do to help?"

With both of us, it took less time than I'd expected. When it came to unhooking the batteries, I was more careful. Call me paranoid, but I spent more time looking for a booby trap than I did unhooking the wires and unscrewing the charge controller.

"This one's done," I said into the PTT mic.

"Copy. We're three minutes out," a voice on the radio said.

"Almost at next checkpoint," Jessica said over the radio. "Watch yourselves, but probably a good time to catch up."

"Copy that," I said. "This one's done. We'll be there shortly."

We'd already mapped out the route, with Jessica and others circling areas they thought they could remember where things were stored. Once we'd gotten these back, along with the batteries, I was going to hook them up and test things out as best as I could, or turn all that over to one of the new guys who was pretty handy with this sort of stuff.

"You ready to ride?" I asked Emily, storing my tools and getting on my quad.

She gave me a salacious smile, then laughed as I felt the heat coming off my skin and my ears turning red.

"I'll never get tired of that," she joked, then fired up her quad, driving off.

I'd never understand what was going on there. I seemed to be a pawn in somebody else's game. I thought about that as we raced down the road to catch up with Jessica. Emily had laid something heavy on me when she'd told me I'd been a sourpuss lately. Things at the homestead were progressing in a good way by leaps and bounds. Adding enough power to have some lights, the well pump, and a fridge running would be game changing if we could pull it off.

I just had to keep an eye out for some good power inverters.

***

"Jessica, Wes, come in." Emily's voice came over the radio.

"Where are you?" I asked into mine.

"Two houses up the road, back at an old barn."

"We don't have to wait for the next truck," Jessica said.

"Ok, I just worry that she wanted to go looking around on her own. Wouldn't take no for an answer."

"I think she wanted to give us time alone," Jessica said. "Not been very much of that lately."

"No, there hasn't been. But there's something I've got to tell you," I said, pulling her close for a quick kiss.

"Something I've been wanting to tell you too," she said, putting her arms on my shoulders.

"Emily and I had a chat, well ... it wasn't a chat, it was more like—"

"She loves you, in her own obsessive way," Jessica said, interrupting my train of thought.

"Yeah, but what I meant to say was..."

"Why are you so flustered? Did something happen?" she asked, an eyebrow arching.

"What? No, I mean, she kissed me on the cheek and told me I should tell you how I really feel."

"Kissed you on the cheek, huh?" Her eyes were twinkling. "I was pretty sure she was going to try to get you alone and..."

"No, nothing like that happened," I told her, grinning.

"Oh, I know. She said she wishes things were different, but she knows we belong together," Jessica told me, leaning in to kiss me again.

"Yeah ... she said I should tell you how much you mean to me," I said after a moment.

"She said that, huh?" She pulled me closer, kissing me again, blanking my mind, and making my hormones scream.

"Yeah, she said life is too short so—"

"Are you guys coming or what? You're really gonna wanna see this," Emily's voice came out of the radio, startling us.

"Sorry," I said, not sure what I was apologizing for, "you uh ... what'd you have to tell me?" I asked her.

"It can wait."

WE FOUND HER QUAD PARKED OUTSIDE A HALF TUMBLED barn. She was sitting on the back, her arms crossed. At first, I thought she was pissed, but as I turned off my quad and got off, I noticed a wicked grin. Giving us alone time? To talk? To have five minutes of adult time? Was it that look she was giving us?

"What'd you find, spunky?" Jessica asked, hopping off and striding toward her, catching up with me.

"Only enough food to keep us supplied for a while," she said, hooking her thumb behind her, pointing to the barn.

Jessica and I ran to the doorway. Underneath what looked like scraps of wood and sheets of ripped tarpaper left over from a roofing project was a small U-Haul trailer. I shot her a puzzled look and picked my way through the fallen boards and debris, avoiding nails, not wanting to get tetanus. The swing doors were open on one side, and boxes of MRE's and bags of grain were stored in there.

"I was killing some time, figuring you two could use a good fifteen or twenty minutes to yourself, so I walked around a bit and came in here, remembering Mary's grandfather's barn, when I saw this. The back lock wasn't closed properly. I was going to see if I could find something to jimmy it open when it came off."

"These are military MREs," Jessica said in wonder.

"And look at those bags of grain? Must be enough in here to last a long time, right?"

I was flabbergasted. Where had this come from, and how had it been missed?

"Yeah." There was about as much in the small covered trailer as I had for food storage for Grandpa and Grandma all in one spot.

"There's so much here, it's flattened the wheels a bit. Overloaded probably."

"I wonder whose it is?" I asked, finally finding words to express my confusion and wonder.

"This looks like somebody stashed this here after FEMA and the cops came through," Jessica said. "Look, there's almost no dust on the trailer. Just dirt from where somebody climbed over it, hiding the front."

"That's what I thought," Emily said quietly, "but because they are military MREs, does that mean FEMA did this, or the Keggers?"

"I don't know," Jessica said, "but having this food would make a world of difference. Did you check the house?"

"Yeah, I knocked on the doors. Front door was open, but this place hasn't been lived in for a couple of years."

"I don't know who lived here," I told Jessica, "actually, I don't recall somebody ever having living here."

"I'm calling it in," she said with a smile.

Emily held her hand up, and I gave her a high five. She waggled her eyebrows at me, then nodded at Jess questioningly as she radioed a change in plans.

"No time," I told her.

"Most guys I know can be done in thirty seconds or less," she said again, making me shake my head.

"Not that, I was trying to talk to her, you pervert."

"Hey, gotta perv while the perving's good. Sometimes all we have are memories. Or fantasies."

"...over," Jessica said, looking at me, grinning.

"Fantasies?" Jessica asked.

"Hey, the nights get lonely. Maybe Mary and I should bunk out in the barn for a couple days, give you two sometime alone?"

"I'd ... like that," Jessica said, turning red in the face.

"Or you could take my spot on the couch," I offered her.

"Hm ... it does smell like you a bit..."

"Are you serious?" I asked her as Jessica busted up laughing.

"Not at all. I just love messing with you. We'll figure things out when we get back home. The last truck can tow this, then you two can have a real date for once."

"Thank you," Jessica said, walking over and giving her a big hug.

Emily wrapped her arms around Jessica's back to return the hug and made an obscene gesture at me. I shook my head at her. Maybe this was how ordinary people acted when put in unordinary situations. They joked around more, the innuendo got thick and deep. There had been a lot more laughter than I'd remembered in the last couple of years, despite everything that had gone on. Maybe it took an apocalypse to bring everyone together. For the first time in a long time, I felt a glimmer of hope shining through the darkness.

22

THE NUMBER of people at the homestead had seemingly increased by a dozen people in the past week, on top of the Gutheries and Jessica's dogs, who were in better shape than the last time I'd seen them. When Linda and Sheriff Jackson got together, they decided to handle security as a team, polling others on their abilities. We found out that we had a guy who'd once worked for an electronics manufacturer in Michigan and knew how to solder. Right away, Jess had pulled out Grandpa's old base station radio and asked him to look at it and get it working. The new solar panels were being tested and were going online as we made sure things worked before tying it all together. We were in search of a large enough inverter to see if we were at a point we could power a fridge, but I hoped we had enough.

The homestead was such a hive of activity that I hardly knew what to do with myself, so when there was nothing to do, I did what I used to. I got one of the turkey fryers out, and on the tenth day after cooking the cornmeal mix, I fired up one of my stills, making sure I had several barrels of water ready to circulate the water. It'd heat up the barn some as I did it, but the days had started to get cooler as summer turned to fall.

I ran almost three barrels of corn mash in a row through the still before Grandpa had me put a stop to it.

"It's good to have this, but we don't need it all right now," he said softly.

"The ladies are using the spent corn to make corn cakes, tortillas, and flatbreads," I pointed out, not wanting him to think I was wasting resources.

"Yeah, but something's gnawing at you, grandson. You're restless, bored. What's going on?"

"They're taking people still," I told him.

"I know, and we're getting information out. After what you did to them and what we did to them when they came here, they've gotten extra careful and upped their defenses like we'd done to ours."

"They've got a lot more people," I told him.

"True, they might," he said, putting his hand on his stomach and wincing, "but that don't mean nothing if they don't hardly leave none."

"How much harm are they doing to the people they've taken?"

"You can't save everyone, least of all by yourself. You're barely healed up now, and you're wanting to go out and start another shooting war?"

"I'd like to go out and start setting up ambushes and whittling them down. Make them chase us and blow the hell out of them. I'd like to—"

"One more week," Grandpa said, putting a finger up. "Wait one more week."

My mouth went dry.

"What happens in one more week?" I asked him.

"The ladies have been working around the clock getting the communications going. The old radio should be finished soon, and Linda knows some way to hook up the new stuff to the old stuff, so it talks to each other. We've started picking up transmissions from the State Police and local government guys and gals. This KGR group isn't anonymous anymore. Everybody is talking about them."

"Then why don't they go after them?" I asked, then regretted the words as I realized how many local police and retired military we had here.

"Outmanned and outgunned," Grandpa said. "Until next week."

"What happens next week?" I asked again, getting frustrated, but smelling the tails of the run start coming out.

I switched jars, marking the end of the run, and waited for his answer.

"How about I let your ladies tell you?" he said, then walked away snickering.

Apparently, everybody assumed I was in a poly relationship. And why was everybody playing coy? Just tell me already. This was the most annoying thing ever. First Jessica, then Emily, Grandpa and—

"Mister Flagg?" Marshall called, walking up.

"Marshall," I said, holding my hand out to shake. "Any word of your cousin?"

As much of a bad guy as Lance was, Marshall had asked everyone with a radio to give him any news of his cousin.

"No, and that's good. No news is good news, right?"

"I think so," I agreed. "What's on your mind?"

"Your grandpa, I overheard him. Um... I think there's about to be a lot more people here than there was a week ago. They have people looking for more beds, lumber, and food and—"

"Whoa, whoa, slow down," I said, seeing the man starting to get a little agitated. "Is this part of the big plan Grandpa was talking about?"

Marshall nodded.

"Well, that's good. There's safety in numbers. You getting enough to eat?" I asked him, knowing it was hard for me to tell. We'd all thinned out on the Post-Apocalyptic Diet, or PAD Diet, as I'd mentally started calling it. The trailer of food helped, but after a while stockpiles of food would run out.

"I just miss..." I expected him to say Lance, "... having someone to talk to."

"But... You're always talking to people. I mean, we're talking?" I was confused, was he being shunned?

"Can I hang out with you and Miss Jessica and Miss

Emily sometime?" he blurted out, turning red in the face.

"Like … a double date?"

He turned even more red.

"You'll have to ask Emily if she'd like to join us," I told him, guessing, since he knew I was already with Jessica, he hadn't bought the poly nonsense.

"No, not a date. I just… I don't have many people close to my age to talk to. It's usually older grown-ups or the little kids."

"You come hang out with us anytime you want, unless there's a hat hanging on the doorknob," I told him with a smile.

"What's the hat on the doorknob mean?" he asked.

"It means," Mary said, walking up, "that him and Miss Jessica are probably talking."

"Oh, well I like talking. Why I can't I be there with the hat on the door?" he asked her.

"Because they're talking with their faces really close," Mary said, mashing her flattened palms together, twisting them, "and I think there's tickle fights, because I hear things and there's giggling. I think he tickles her."

"All right," Emily said, walking up in the doorway, probably hearing the last of it. "I think that's enough talking for you."

"But, Mom, Marshall is my friend, I was just trying to—"

Emily made her scurry off, apologizing for her daughter. She came in and sat on the straw bale next to

Marshall who had sat in my chair. Jessica stood in the doorway, a confused look on her face for a moment, only having caught the last bit.

"Hm... I see, I guess," Marshall said after a pregnant silence.

"You understand now?" Emily asked, having been clued in on Marshall's innocent nature.

"Yeah, and see, Miss Emily, it's not a date, but I'd like to hang out with you, Jessica, and Wes, and maybe we could, I mean you and me, could have a tickle fight someday?"

If I didn't have the still running hot, I might have died right there. Jessica flopped in Grandpa's chair behind me and pulled me backward, almost off my feet, so I was sitting on her, squishing her.

"You ticklish, big boy?" she asked, and then proceeded to find out while everyone burst into laughter.

I got up after Jessica claimed I was going to pinch her bladder shut and went back and switching jars again, turning off the burner. I snickered at the innocent way Marshall had somewhat asked Emily out, oblivious about the double entendre that had been created by a six-year-old. The girls started chatting, Jessica asking stories about Mary when she was little.

Marshall stood suddenly. "So it's ok if I hang out with you guys like this?"

"You're more than welcome to hang out with us anytime," Emily told him.

"Thank you. Maybe someday we'll talk more about that tickle fight, Miss Emily, see ya."

We waited half a heartbeat then I busted up again, watching the short, savage woman turn red in the face. Jessica was only half a second behind me in laughter. Emily held out long enough for Marshall to leave the barn and leaned forward, putting her hands over her face, her laughter making her whole body convulse and her eyes leak at the edges.

"He's really kind of cute," she said after a moment, wiping her eyes.

"Oh, girl, your influence would corrupt him," Jessica said, play slapping at her arm.

"Only where it counts," she shot back.

Oh man. I had to get out of here. The cooler night air was calling to me. I remembered what Marshall was saying about Grandpa and next week. I turned to go back into the shine room, but overheard what Emily and Jessica were talking about and turned tail and almost ran. Apparently, the locker room talk I'd heard growing up and in college was rather tame compared to the whispered words I overheard. My face was turning red just hearing Jessica recounting what had happened on that straw bale, in more explicit detail than an adult magazine would print.

23

I FINALLY MADE Grandpa tell me over dinner what was coming. The State Police had gotten together again and had been doing a lot of what we'd been doing, and setting up a regional communications center with scavenged materials. The Sheriff's Departments from all the counties had been checking in, and for our county, our homestead was the base of operations. Old uniforms had been dragged out and cleaned. They would be used for day to day law operations, but most of the guys wore their Mossy Oak or camouflage BDUs when working on securing our area.

Spider and Henry's men were locusts on the countryside and there had been skirmishes with them and other groups. I wasn't the only one they had a beef with, apparently. The State boys had gone out in force, 20 men, to stop a suspected raid. Somebody in Henry's group near the bunker had been feeding information, but Linda, Jessica and the Gutheries hadn't known who it was, and they were only transmitting by scramble to the State Police.

To top things off, in the short space of time, other groups and communities had come together as people had escaped the camps, citing food shortages, sanitation going to hell and rampant sickness brought on from people being massed together. The government had been doing all it could, but wasn't chasing those who left with any heart. Still, it killed me to know people were getting preyed on, but we were powerless to do anything.

Spider hadn't just brought in an extra hundred guys, he'd put the call out over secured communications for any in his organization to come and meet with them. Henry and Spider had had this planned a long time ago. We learned Henry had once worked as a contractor for Spider, doing IT and communications. The big secret people had been tiptoeing about? The State Police, another likeminded group of Three Percenter's and ours were planning a massive get-together and raid on the new compound where the RVs had been parked, 20 miles east of Delight, Arkansas.

Linda would be going, but Jessica and I were asked to stay behind to help with the home defenses while they were conducting the raid. Apparently there were a lot of police and former military going. Somebody like me, who had no formal training, would just get in the way. I didn't like it, but if I wasn't going to be there, I was glad to have my entire family, Jessica, Emily and

Mary, with me. Diesel had been fighting an on again and off again infection. Without antibiotics it wasn't easy, and keeping his wound clean so he could heal was a job entirely left to Jessica, as nobody else wanted to get in the way of the big dog.

"So, today's the day?" Grandma asked, sliding some pan-fried corn mush and onions cooked up like hash browns onto my plate with the three eggs I usually ate.

"Yes ma'am. In about an hour, Grandpa, Jessica and I are going to be taking turns checking the defenses and I'll be ranging ahead a little bit. I've got some more thermite to lay out some more surprises."

"Lester's going too," Grandma said with a harrumph.

A banging sound and cursing came out of Grandma's bedroom as Grandpa got ready. A lot of the plate carriers stripped from Spider's men had been rinsed, washed as well as they could be, and given to the men going on the raid today. A lot of them had vests already, but some of the former military didn't, and anything that could stop a bullet would be a blessing. What worried us was the mounted fifty caliber machine guns that the group had seemingly acquired. I'd been told they had an effective range of almost a mile. They could walk bullets in, adjusting their aim. That gave a lot of us sleepless nights, but they'd have to have some kind of line of sight. With us being in a hollow area between ridges we were pretty protected, but it was something we'd been planning to defend against.

Some fertilizer, some fuel oil, and a few sticks of

dynamite had been staged in areas where old steel drums had been dropped off on our side of the road. You needed a good solid primary explosive to set off ANFO, and dynamite was the preferred method of 'shooting' a charge like that off. I knew it in theory, but the IED guy from the middle east wars had been in charge of that. He was collecting copper to make a cone shaped charge. He didn't know how to cast it, so for now, he just planned on using the ANFO to use barrel bombs.

"Hey Grandma!" Jessica said, walking in and sitting down next to me.

"Have you eaten dear?" she asked sweetly, happy to see us together again.

"I will in a second," she said, stealing my fork and taking a big bite. "Mmffis is good," she said around a mouthful.

"I'm wounded, food from my own mouth?"

She bumped my hip with hers, a feat I couldn't have done without spilling out of the chair, then gave me my fork back.

"My stomach was sour, but Mom ate, and this smelled good. Better hurry, we have to leave in ten."

"I thought we were going in an hour?" I asked her.

"You and I are ranging ahead. Somebody has to be far eyes for this operation, and make sure communications at the farm are kept up to date in case the radios don't work that far. So, you got your choice. Four-wheeler or bikes?"

"Is there a bad guy within five miles of us?" I asked

her, knowing she'd been sitting near the communications center in the barn almost nonstop when she wasn't with me.

"Nope." She smiled and pulled a piece of fried corn mush off my fork with her fingers just as I was trying to take a bite, popping it into her mouth, "Now I took food out of your mouth."

I sighed. "Wait, we can't take the dogs if we take the four wheelers."

"We'll need them," Jessica said, "Diesel should be good to go behind me on one of the four wheelers. Raider and Yaeger can either ride with you or run along. We don't have to break land speed records or anything."

She reached for my plate again, but I was ready, trapping her hand. Raider grumbled from under the table, and Yaeger or Diesel barked from outside.

"I've got some stuff I want to bring. More of the Tannerite mix like I'd used at the Crater. It'll have to be wrapped up good, so it doesn't jiggle too badly."

"Will it blow up?" she asked, though I was sure she knew the answer.

"Doubt it, they're in glass jars. Going to put them at the base of trees. We see a bad guy coming in a truck, shoot the yellow stripes and hopefully drop a tree on them, in front of them or behind them."

"Why behind them?" she asked, an eyebrow arched.

"So, they can't escape." I grinned, starting to eat.

"I love to see you two lovebirds discussing murder

and mayhem so early in the morning. Now when am I getting some damn grandkids?"

Jessica had stolen my mug of coffee and was taking a drink when Grandma spoke, and she started coughing. I laughed and pounded her on the back the same way I had Mary not too long ago.

"Where are the kids and everyone going?" I asked Grandma.

"Well, if they weren't worried about the raid going wrong and being chased all the way back here, how about the next county to the west of us?" I asked.

"Back of the property," Jessica said, "near the marshy spot."

"About that..." Grandma was hesitant.

"What?" Jessica asked.

"Tell the ladies and kids not to pick anything new that might be growing back there before you leave. Can't miss it if they're going back there."

"Grandma!" I said, a little shocked.

"Well, this kind of thing takes time, and the plants shouldn't be ready until after we get our first frost. They finish really fast."

I rolled my eyes and kept eating as Grandpa walked out of the back room, wearing his poaching gear, and carrying his suppressed rifle.

"Good," I said nodding in agreement with his armament and clothing choices. "Will you tell the kids and ladies who are going to the back of the property not to pick Grandma's new garden?"

Grandpa snickered, but he was nodding, "You

leaving one of the hounds with us here when you both take off?"

"I... actually, that's not a bad idea," I told him. "You got your choice, Diesel or Raider," I said.

"Yeah, Diesel will listen to your grandpa. I can give him a command to stay and protect and he'll do his job 'til we get back."

"Man bear pig it is," Grandpa said walking out.

"Man bear pig?" Jessica asked.

"Cartoons have rotted his brain," I said cryptically, finishing my plate off in record time.

"And what plants? New garden?"

"I'll tell you on the way. Let's fill our canteens and get going."

Jessica sighed, but nodded.

———

"RADIO CHECK," A STRANGE VOICE SAID ON THE CHANNEL today's raid was using.

"Got you loud and clear. Targets in sight?"

They weren't using normal radio etiquette. I smiled, listening.

"Jessica, you want to help me set some of these up while we listen to what's going on?" I asked her, placing anther Tannerite charge.

"Sure. Any particular pattern?"

"No, but it wouldn't hurt to have some of the trip ones Grandpa rigged set out, would it?"

"I wouldn't, unless all of our people know about it.

Right now, these are just yellow painted jars of powder to anybody who didn't know any better. Wouldn't want one of the kids picking berries to set it off."

I winced, then nodded, then had an evil thought. "You know what?" I asked her/ "What about grand babies?"

She threw a stick at me. "You're really not funny."

"I'm not?"

"No. You know what hasn't happened since our first date?"

"A real second, third, fourth and fifth date?" I asked her, confused.

She let out a groan and took another jar and walked away, Yaeger following her. I turned to Raider, "Buddy, do you know what she's talking about?"

He cocked his head to the side, then the other direction. Great, even the dog wasn't going to fill me in. I set the last jar I had out and debated walking back to the four-wheeler. We were done here for now.

"Raider, you ready for us to fall back some?" I asked him.

He barked once and ran to the Four-Trax Honda I'd kept for myself. It wasn't the swiftest of quads, but it had wide luggage racks. I had a blanket down in the back of the larger rack for Raider to sit down on. He jumped up there, completely avoiding knocking off my backpack, and lay down in his spot. I played musical shoulder harnesses and slings while I put my pack on and waited for Jessica. I saw Yaeger come running down the side of the ditch, stopping next to the red quad she'd picked for herself. A moment later, Jessica came, and he got on the quad.

Whatever had bugged her earlier seemed to be gone, and she had a slight smile on her face.

"They've all moved into position. Going to wait until dusk to hit them," she said, tapping the radio, her rifle slung over her shoulder.

"Ready to head back to Grandma's cooking?" I asked her, knowing we still had a couple hours left on our patrol/watch.

"I am kind of hungry. I had a light snack a sec ago of some tail mix, but I haven't been feeling good."

"You look ok now?" I asked getting off the quad and walking over to her.

I put both hands on her temples and pulled her close, kissing her forehead. She wrapped her arms around my neck and held me as I planted another kiss on her temple and then pushed back. Too much of that and we'd have clothing strung along the trail forever, and I had no idea how far away the next set of eyes was. Being mature sucked sometimes.

"I feel ok right now, it's just in the mornings that my stomach has been bugging me."

I looked at her cheek for any signs of infection, the turned her head the other way with my thumb under her chin. She let me, even though I knew she could probably have broken me in half if she wanted. The stitches had come out a while back, but I didn't see anything on the outside that gave the sign of infection. No angry red lines leading away from the scars.

243

"Is your tooth bugging you?" I asked her.

"No, it's not that. Don't worry, let's just get back to our post."

"Yes ma'am," I said giving her a mock salute, turning.

I was rewarded with a slap on the ass. I spun around just as she fired up the quad, revving it, then she took off down the road, Yaeger sitting behind her like he'd been riding like that forever.

DUSK DIDN'T FALL QUICKLY. IT WAS GRADUAL IN coming. We had the radio on, sitting side by side in a wooden barricade half a mile from the homestead, acting as advance warning as it was one of the higher spots along this particular road, and the radios worked well here. It was still hot under the camou-flaged tarp, but there was enough light coming from the stacked deadfall that I could make out her features, and the dogs sleeping in the pile of leaves next to us.

"It's almost time," Jessica said quietly.

"I know, I've been praying this goes off good."

"Wes, there's something I want you to know—"

I was turning to face her when the radio went off. "Now."

There were ticking sounds coming out of the radio as everyone confirmed. A pause of twenty seconds to see if anybody at the compound had cracked their codes and had been listening in. Nobody made a sound.

"Let's light 'em up," somebody said over the radio.

"Looks like they started," Jessica said to me.

I reached over and grabbed her free hand, giving it a squeeze. She squeezed back, then let it go as the sound of a motor fired up somewhere in the distance.

"Grandpa, you fire up the tractor?" I asked into my handset.

"Nope," Grandpa said. "Keep the line clear, might be incoming."

That was what I was afraid of. From where we were sitting, we could get to the farm in a hurry, but if somebody was coming this way, we were either in the right spot, or they were coming in the other way; in which case we'd have to really burn rubber to try to get there to make any sort of difference. The radio I was using was tuned into the frequency the homestead was using, while Jessica's was plugged into the tactical network that was being used for the raid. My radio went off.

"Silent Hunter, this is Kathy Bates, you copy?" Emily's voice came out of the radio.

I shuddered. "I copy, please don't use the axe, Annie, please."

"You still getting the motor sounds?"

"Yes, it's faint. Sounded like it was close when it first started up, but I can hardly hear it now."

"That's because the woman from Misery is talking to you on the radio," Jessica said softly.

"Sounded like it came from your direction, just trying to triangulate. Over."

"Ok, sounds like the sound did originate in this direction." I ran my mental map on where everyone was. Emily was working with a younger couple who'd come in a week back, but they were west of the homestead a good hundred yards; we were east of there a good half a mile. "Will check back in."

"Any updates on the tactical net?" Over?

"Nothin—"

The roar of a motor was loud all of a sudden, and it wasn't further down the road from us; it sounded like it was coming down the road right on top of us. Jessica and I turned as one. The dogs were alarmed enough that they took off out of the shelter barking. It took me half a second, but I yanked the tarp off of us as we had been trying to do the same thing at once and working against each other. Now that it was off, in the dusk I could see headlights bouncing down the hill a good two hundred feet away.

"Somebody's driving through the trees!" Jessica called, panicked.

"Anybody at the homestead expecting a big vehicle?"

"Not ours," Grandpa said tersely.

I had two jars of Tannerite between where the vehicle was coming through and where we were.

"Knock some trees down," I screamed, lined up my sight, and slowly squeezed the trigger at the far jar.

This was going to be tricky. It was nearly full dark

now, and I could barely see the jars. If it wasn't for the yellow spray paint, I never would have seen them. We shot at the same time, apparently at the same target. The explosion was immediate, sending dirt and rocks into the air with a huge white and blue tinged cloud. I couldn't tell if the tree was down or not, but as I was lining up on the second tree to fire, Jessica was already firing. This one was even closer than the last, and chunks of something went flying past my head.

Raider ran to my side, and although my ears were ringing, I couldn't see or hear the vehicle. I imagined him making a nervous growling sound, I knew I probably was.

"With me," Jessica said, smacking my shoulder, and took off at a dead run diagonally up the hill. Yaeger was already on her heels. I must not have been that deafened, I heard that, but when I started running toward the area we'd shot, Raider followed.

That was when I heard the buzz saw open up. The muzzle flashes made it easy to see where the vehicle was. It wasn't shooting in our direction, but the flashes blinded me, nonetheless. Jessica grabbed my shoulder and yanked me behind a large tree. I pulled Raider in close to me and tried to get him to hold still. He was still barking and wouldn't listen to me trying to shush him. Maybe his ears were ringing the same way mine were.

I put my hand around his muzzle, while the other was holding onto the sling of my rifle and his collar. He fought and tried to pull backward, but I used my weight and strength. If he went out there, he'd be a moving target. I had an idea Jessica wanted us to hide before the smoke cleared. I saw she was doing the same with Yaeger, who hated being muzzled as much as my pup did. Raider started shaking his head from side to side, almost breaking my grip, and I had to drop the rifle and redouble my efforts. A tree crashed and snapped as the engine roared again. The firing stopped, and the cordite and homemade Tannerite added to a cloudy funky smell.

"If you settle down and be quiet, I'll really let you eat Foghorn," I told Raider, almost nose to nose with the struggling dog.

His body shook, and his legs trembled, but he quit thrashing and pushed against my hand and onto my lap. If he couldn't scare off the big thing, he'd smother me with love and protect me that way. I reached to the edge of the tree and pulled my rifle close. I knew I'd have to check the barrel for obstructions, but right now, I willed myself to be as still and silent as could be. That was when the lights snapped on.

I could see the outline of some kind of armored vehicle. It had a main gun that chilled me to the bone. I didn't know if it was a .50 caliber machine gun, or a 25mm cannon. It looked huge, and it'd just completely destroyed the wooden barrier we had been hiding behind. I could see a gunner standing exposed, both hands on the gun, looking side to side with some kind of night or thermal optics over his face. He pushed those up, now probably blinded by the lights. Raider whined, so I rubbed his head with one hand, but still didn't release the collar.

"...check?"

"Nothing survived that." Two voices were shouting at each other from the APC.

It wasn't an armored Hummer either. It had six wheels, with the front end of it shaped like a wedge. I heard Jess and turned to see her whispering madly into her radio. I felt for the PTT earpiece and found the end and plugged in my radio then turned up the volume. The gunner pushed himself up by his arms and stood on the top of the APC while somebody handed him a rifle.

"Silent Hunter, I repeat, Silent—" Grandpa's voice.

"I'm here," I said into the radio, talking over his transmission.

"Report," a different voice said. The IED guy?

"Some kind of APC, with what looks like a belt fed heavy machine gun on top."

"Is the turret armored or covered? How many wheels?"

"Not covered, six wheels. Over."

"Six wheels, do any of you have a grenade or few to drop in the hatch?"

The gunner dropped to the ground and started walking over to the wooden barrier we'd been hiding behind. In a few moments he'd see we weren't there. We had to do something. That thing would take out the homestead on its own! How did it get past all sets of eyes on Spider's people? I feared the answer was simple. They were better than us.

"No grenades," I said softly, wondering if the gunner's ears were ringing as hard as mine were.

"Just the one vehicle?" Grandpa's voice cut in.

"Yeah," I whispered.

"Lester, if you hear me, get some ninety-five percent in some glass bottles and rags. I need to go to my powder room. Do you copy?"

"Got to drop it straight in," the other voice who'd been asking me questions said.

"I got a pretty damned good idea what I'm doing, son," Grandpa said. "Make sure somebody takes out the gunner before they get close to the homestead. I'm taking a group of us old boys and will be heading up hill 300 yards. You pansies better be ready for fireworks."

24

JESSICA WAS FURIOUSLY WHISPERING into her own headset. I let go of Raider and raised my carbine up, sighting in on the black clad ninja wannabe. I was about to fire when Jessica pulled on my shoulder. I turned to look at her, hoping my movements didn't give us away in the smoky gloom.

"It carries nine people. They'll just open fire on us here when somebody pops up."

"We can't let it get to the homestead," I said, raising the rifle again.

"We need some kind of explosive or Molotov—"

"Grandpa is opening up his powder room, and Les is getting some pure shine ready to throw," I told her.

"Dynamite?"

"That and then some," I told her, shuddering.

"Wait, the barrel bombs..." Jessica's face lit up.

"I'm sure they thought of that, but—"

"Sit tight until they start moving again. In the darkness we can get behind them, and unless somebody in the back is wearing thermal and looking straight out a port, they'll never see us. We'll have to go on foot, because the quads might give us away—"

"There's nothing here," The gunner yelled.

I let out a deep breath as he turned and jogged to the APC and climbed on. "They probably don't have enough people available to cover all positions now that they've committed." He was still yelling, and, with the open turret, I was sure that, unless they were all wearing ear protection, they were just as deafened still.

"Teams one through four pull back to the south side," a voice crackled in the earpiece I was wearing.

"Plans A, B, C are a go," Grandpa said into the radio.

"Be safe," I whispered into the mic.

"The news gets worse," Jessica said to me as the APC's engine roared, making the humongous vehicle lurch forward, until it was rolling down the dirt road away from us.

"Is your mom ok?" I asked her.

"Yeah," she said softly, watching the lights disappear in the gloom, "but they were waiting for them. They..." her voice hitched, and she took in a couple of shuddering breaths. "It's not good, it's really not good."

As heartless as my next words were, we needed to get moving, "Your mom is fine, so let's follow along so we aren't too late—"

"We can't get too close. I don't know what plan C is, but A and B are the barrel bombs."

I reached over to key up the mic, but Jess stopped me. "They must be in on our comms somehow."

I cursed and nodded. "How long do we wait?"

"For the first two explosions. We can't get too close, or the blast will kill us."

DARKNESS BECAME LIGHT, AND THE BUZZ SAW OF THE heavy machine gun ripped the silence of the darkness to shreds. The APC had been driving slow enough that the four of us could keep their lights in sight by jogging, and we happened to be on top of the hill. We crested another one to see the tail end of a massive fireball and the muzzle flashes from the APC and the north side of the roadway. The machine gun fell silent.

"Got him," I yelled, pumping my fist.

I spoke too soon; the engine revved up, and this time the APC moved with real speed. Maybe the gunner had ducked, or he'd been replaced.

"We think they're on our comms and have intel on our defenses," I said suddenly into the mic, thinking to mention that.

The utter insanity of the situation had me wishing we had normal technology, and we could all have been in on a group Skype chat or something. Constant information, constant feedback.

"Plan B adjusting," a voice said in the radio, "and ready."

A moment later, we took off at a run as a massive

blast shook the night, even bigger and more impressive than the first. The shockwave displaced a lot of air, enough for us to feel and smell the heat and chemical fire.

"It's still moving," a woman's voice said over the radio.

"Didn't work," I said, starting to run. "We need to hurry."

"Less talk, more running," Jess said as we took off at a dead run.

"It's stopped," Grandpa said in the radio. "Plan c in place?"

"Shut up and throw, old man," Lester called, loud enough for us to hear.

In the darkness I saw a dozen flaming bottles arc through the air. More than half sailed right over the edge of the APC, a few hit the side, and one hit right in front of the gunner. With horror, I watched as he turned and started spraying the side of the road, the tracers looking like laser beams.

"No!" I screamed, firing at the exposed gunner at the same time as Jess. We were too far out, but we kept moving as we fired single shots. Our ricochets off the armor showed us our misses, but as good of a shot as I was, I wasn't trained in moving and shooting as fast as I was.

The gunner turned and started spraying the north

side of the road when an explosion on top of the tank made the gun fall silent.

"Grandson, I love you," Grandpa said over the radio. "If you get eyes on a ball of sticky in a moment or two, shoot it."

"Grandpa, what are you—"

"Reload," Jessica said, bumping me, almost making me trip over Raider.

More flaming bottles arced in the air, the spreading fire from the nearly pure ethanol engulfing the APC, spreading to the dirt road and the brush on either side of it. Jessica was right, I had to focus; the gunner didn't realize we were twenty seconds away from breathing right down his neck. I dropped the magazine and kept running while pulling out a full one from my pouch and letting the bolt slam shut.

I stopped suddenly, willing Jessica not to get in my sight. I let my breath out slowly, my sights on the man's neck, just above his vest, and slowly squeezed the trigger. The world seemed to slow down. I could almost see the bullet as it left the barrel. I watched it take what felt like two or three seconds to fly through while he was spraying the defenders on the side of the road, bullets blowing chunks of wood and dirt sky high. My bullet nearly tore the base of the man's skull off as it hit the top of his neck. The machine gun sputtered for a second longer, then went silent.

"There's more inside!" Jessica screamed.

We weren't at the homestead yet, but a short run and we'd be there, which meant all the innocents were in range of that gun. The gunner's body was pulled from sight, and a set of hands grabbed the top of the APC to pull themselves up. Jessica and I poured on the fire as something exploded in front of the armored vehicle, clouding my shot with smoke. I cursed and started running again, to catch up with Jessica who'd taken cover behind a tree on the south side of the road. My dog? Where was my dog? I looked around frantically, but my attention was drawn ahead once more when another explosion lit the night up under one of the wheels.

I was almost deafened at this point, barely hearing that one, waiting for the smoke to clear enough to get a shot. Ignoring the flames licking the side of the metal, two or three figures climbed the APC and dropped something inside of it and ran like hell. The smoke cleared enough for me to see Grandpa's form. He wasn't fast, and he was running like he was in great pain. I silently cheered him on when a head popped up from inside the APC, holding what looked like a big ball of duct tape in one hand and a pistol in the other. He raised his gun to fire.

I snapped off two quick shots just as he started firing, and he ducked down, trying to dislodge the wad of tape. Jessica opened up the same time I did, forcing his head out of sight. The engine of the APC roared, and it backed up, giving the mounted gun more maneuverability. The figure popped up again, and he appeared to be wearing some sort of mask and helmet in addition to his vest. He tried to throw the ball of tape again but couldn't. I remembered Grandpa's words and sighted on that and slowed down my breathing, letting my breath out, clicking the carbine on 'pew, pew, pew' and gently squeezed until a three round burst surprised the hell out of me.

I saw sparks from the first two misses against the armor, but the last round hit the ball of tape. The explosion ... it was huge, and it set something off inside the APC. More explosions went off, muffled inside the armor, then the whole night lit up. The ammunition stores started cooking off, and we hit the deck as people poured concentrated fire at the APC from the south side of the driveway, the bullets ricocheting around Jessica and me.

"Where are the dogs?" I asked, making sure I was behind the same tree she was.

"They ran to the homestead's direction," she shouted back to me.

25

"Westley," Grandma's voice cut through the night.

She used a tone of voice that I'd never heard. It was fear, anger and sorrow mixed together.

"I'm coming, Grandma," I screamed, running as hard as I could, forgetting the unknown danger.

My chest expanded as even more adrenaline dumped into my bloodstream, my lungs expanding to hold more air. I didn't have far to go, but time had slowed still, and it was taking me forever to get there. I didn't know if Jessica was following me still or if she was looking for other invaders. I didn't care, when Grandma called, you came. When Grandma sounded like that when she called, you dropped everything.

"Hurry!" Her voice was shrill.

"Has anybody heard from Linda and Sheriff Jackson?" I asked, my heart heavy.

"No," Emily said softly.

Mary, Emily, Grandma and Raider were sitting at the kitchen table while I made coffee in the percolator. Breakfast had been eggs, fried corn mush, and leftover cornbread from last night. I'd already served them food, but I had forgotten to put the percolator on the cooktop. Jessica had left the day after the funeral services at the farm.

"I'm going to miss Grandpa," Mary said quietly.

"I know, sweetie," Emily said, shooting a look my and Grandma's way, probably to ensure we wouldn't break out weeping. It was a close thing.

I walked over and wrapped my arms around Grandma's shoulders, hugging her tightly.

"Why did he get in so close?" I asked her softly.

"Mary dear, how about you go find Marshall and ask him to start story time early?" Grandma asked.

"But I don't—"

"Mary," Emily said softly, "listen to Grandma."

We waited until she pulled her shoes on and left the house before Grandma indicated for me to sit.

"Grandpa knew if that big gun got close ... there was nothing we have here that could have stopped it. We were listening in when you called that the top of the gunner's spot wasn't covered. He ... the grenades were that bomb guy's idea. Got them from the fourteen we buried, but those didn't work. Grandpa had some dynamite and that stuff you made left in his powder room. After he told a few of the home guard how to make them, they did. He knew they had to get it right in the hole..."

"But why him?" I asked her.

"He didn't want to die, Westley, but the cancer was coming back—"

"You can't know that," I told her. "He was feeling better."

"No," Grandma said, "he had all the signs of before —and worse."

Emily was silent, and I thought about her words. What she was saying ... how could I have missed that? Was I really as blind as the ladies thought I was? Wait ... how he was walking and moving; I'd chalked it up to usual aches and pains from overdoing things, but that hadn't been the case.

"It was back in his innards. He didn't want you to know." Her words were quiet.

"I've helped him around a time or two when Grandma wasn't around," Emily told me.

"You knew?" More anger than I expected came out.

"No, but I saw. I didn't know him the way you guys do, but I could tell he was in pain."

"But why would he—"

"He knew he didn't have long and did what he had to do. He knew you wouldn't miss." A tear rolled down her cheek. "He told me before he went out to the road-side that he was at peace, and he was proud of you."

Something in my chest I'd been holding back cut loose, and the tears came. Again. That last racking of the machine gun had caught Lester, Grandpa, and another half dozen defenders. The death was quick, they'd told me. I wasn't allowed to see him until we were burying him. Emily had seen to the dead while I sat inside with Grandma and Mary. Jessica did what she could, but her mother hadn't checked in after the firefight. She feared the worst and had insisted on going alone. To find her mother, and to find out if there were any more survivors.

She hadn't wanted me to go with her, but she'd taken her dogs. Diesel had mostly healed from his ordeal. Our lives had been thrown together, ripped apart, thrown together again and now? I didn't know. I hurt all over, and it wasn't from any physical pain inside of me. Outside, Raider was chasing the chickens, and Foghorn let out a very un-rooster like sound as Raider almost caught him. Grandma looked up, watching the kids chase the dog, the dog chase the chickens, the chickens chasing after the kids for any snacks or treats.

"Marshall said it's too early." Mary walked in and wrapped her little arms around my chest, hugging me.

"It'll be ok," she said.

"Thank you," I told her, kissing the top of her head, hugging her back.

The radio that was on the counter made a sound, then Jessica's voice came out of the static.

"Silent Hunter, this is Yaeger's mom. You copy?"

The radio started going nuts as everyone with a radio at the farm got on the horn at once, asking about loved ones. I knew I wasn't going to talk over the chatter with this radio, so I took off at a dead run for the barn. People saw me coming and moved. I got in just as somebody was sitting in front of the radio. I grabbed the headphones and put them on, snatching the mic away from the startled woman.

"Sorry, she's calling me," I said, then keyed up the mic. "Silent Hunter here. Did you find the packages?"

"Yes," Jessica's voice said, sounding relieved. "More than we'd initially thought. Had to go radio silent for search and then bugout. Will you be ready for deliveries?"

"Yes, Yaeger's mom, copy that. ETA?"

"For me to know and you to find out." Her words were annoying, but I caught a tone of relief.

"Yaeger's mom, you're going to owe me."

The rest of the folks who had been clamoring to talk to Jessica had been trampled over with my transmissions, as the base unit had a lot more power and the big antenna to push signal farther. They had given up and gone silent as Jessica and I had been talking.

"I'll fix you some dinner, just as soon as... CONTACT—"

Gunfire came out of the speaker as somebody near her started screaming, then the transmission cut off.

.   .   .

-THE END -

TO BE NOTIFIED OF NEW RELEASES, PLEASE SIGN UP FOR my mailing list at: http://eepurl.com/bghQbɪ--

ABOUT THE AUTHOR

Boyd Craven III was born and raised in Michigan, an avid outdoorsman who's always loved to read and write from a young age. When he isn't working outside on the farm, or chasing a household of kids, he's sitting in his Lazy Boy, typing away.

You can find the rest of Boyd's books on Amazon & Select Book Stores.

boydcraven.com
boyd3@live.com

Printed in Great Britain
by Amazon

18961042R00157